I AM
GOD

GIACOMO SARTORI

I AM
GOD

Translated from the Italian
by Frederika Randall

RESTLESS BOOKS
BROOKLYN, NEW YORK

First published as *Sono Dio* by NN Editore, Milan

First Restless Books paperback edition March 2019

A slightly different version of chapters 1 to 3 appeared
in the *Massachusetts Review*, vol 58, no 4.

Paperback ISBN: 9781632062147

Library of Congress Control Number: 2018948327

Cover design by Adam B. Bohannon
Cover illustration by Eugenia Loli

Set in Garibaldi by Tetragon, London
Printed in Canada

1 3 5 7 9 10 8 6 4 2

Restless Books, Inc.
232 3rd Street, Suite A111
Brooklyn, NY 11215

www.restlessbooks.org
publisher@restlessbooks.org

For Piuma Lange,
who having passed on a weakness for the page,
then bequeathed me her indomitable fragility.

Is it not a paradox that the Christian Religion has in large part been the source of atheism or more generally of religious unbelief? Yet I think that is the case. Man is not naturally incredulous because he does not reason much and does not care a great deal about the causes of things.

GIACOMO LEOPARDI, *ZIBALDONE*
MICHAEL CAESAR AND FRANCO D'INTINO, EDS.

Whatever their religious affinities, many today don't seek a God they can comprehend rationally, to whom they address themselves as to a person. They seek a more mysterious, more impersonal God, one that eludes the human intellect.

FRÉDÉRIC LENOIR,
LES MÉTAMORPHOSES DE DIEU

CONTENTS

I AM
GOD

I HAVE NO NEED TO THINK

I AM GOD. Have been forever, will be forever. *Forever*, mind you, with the razor-sharp glint of a diamond, and without any counterpart in the languages of men. When a man says, *I'll love you forever*, everyone knows that *forever* is a frail and flimsy speck of straw in the wind. A vow that won't be kept, or that in any case is very unlikely to be kept. A lie, in other words. But when I say forever, I really do mean forever. So let that be clear.

I am God, and I have no need to think. Up to now I've never thought, and I've never felt the need, not in the slightest. The reason human beings are in such a bad way is because they think; thought is by definition sketchy and imperfect—and misleading. To any thought one can oppose another, obverse thought, and to that yet another, and so forth and so on; and this inane cerebral yakety-yak is about as far from divine as you can get. Every thought is destined to expire from the moment it's hatched, just like the mind that hatched it. A god does not think—that's the last thing we need!

A spiral galaxy is a spiral galaxy, a white dwarf is a white dwarf, a platyhelminth of the class turbellaria is a platyhelminth, class turbellaria, while I on the other hand am God. These are the facts. Don't ask me how I came to be God, because I myself have no idea. Or rather I do know, just as I know everything, but it would take eons to put into words, and quite frankly, I don't think it's worth it. My rank (let's call it that) alone guarantees a certain degree of credibility.

A god does not watch, does not wait, does not listen. Does not feed, crave, or belch. A god is engaged in something human language cannot express, composed of all the actions (and all the non-actions) that all the languages together can pronounce, but also all those inexpressible in words. And thus surpasses both the first and the second. You might say that a god *is*, if only the verb "to be" were a pale shadow of my real existence (call it that), which is above all *sense*. I am the meaning of everything.

Of course the platyhelminth and the Sun, which as everyone knows is a yellow dwarf, are in some ways also divine, given that I created them. If someone were to call them God I certainly wouldn't be offended. But if many past civilizations considered the sun a god, so far as I know not even the most radical animists among humans ever made a divinity of a necrophagous worm. I wish someone would explain to me why; the way I see it, there's no reason at all why a paltry little star (the *sun*) can be a supreme being, and the platyhelminth, no. I mean, we need to talk about this. But for simplicity's sake (start nitpicking here and we'll never get anywhere), think of me as distinct from the red dwarfs and the platyhelminths. Think of me as God, period. Anyone can picture God.

I myself don't even know what made me decide to speak (or more properly, write). No one forced me, it wasn't a question of burning need, I wasn't feeling lonely, didn't have anything to give vent to, or to hand down. Wasn't bored, didn't feel a desire to hear (as it were) my own voice. Wasn't in search of a new experience (for me, a meaningless expression), wasn't hoping to become a media star (the latter-day Paradise that humans now lust after). Wasn't even seeking to be understood. God has no need of such trifles. So let us say: I do not know. In truth, omniscience means that I do know. It would require about ten interactive encyclopedias with billions of entries and cross-entries to explain the matter with enough clarity and simplicity so that humans could understand (humans are not all that smart), but it could be done. I just don't see the point of such a hermeneutic exercise.

SODOMATRIX ON A BIKE

A GOD does infinite things, as everyone knows, but at the same time, paradoxical as it may seem, a god has nothing particular to do. He's no layabout, but neither is he a bean counter punching a time card morning and night, and even less a workaholic. He does what he must without stress and without fatigue, without making too much of it. In some ways without even being aware of it. A god in the first instance is simply busy being god. He watches, he listens, although his watching and listening have nothing in common with that of humans. *I am god*, he thinks.

I contemplate, I listen. I observe, for example, the galaxy called the *Milky Way*, and more precisely what is called the *Solar System*, and even more precisely, the planet *Earth*. My eyes (if you know what I mean) fall on a very tall girl (everything's relative) in a high-tech cowshed, the polar opposite of a bucolic nativity scene. I see her introduce her gloved hand into a cow's anus and with a rapid rotary motion of the wrist, extract a handful of feces the consistency of mud from the big rectum. She then cleans off the animal's swollen vulva, spreads it open and inserts the point of an instrument that looks in some ways like a syringe, in other ways like a handgun, pushing to penetrate the beast and rotating her hand from time to time. Then she once again sticks her left fist up the backside, this time following through with the entire arm, right past the elbow. The way you might lean way over to pick up some object that has fallen behind the sofa.

I really can't explain why, among the many, not to say infinite, possibilities out there, my gaze always seems to come to rest on the Milky Way. And why within the Milky Way, which is really not so tiny, my sights are trained on the Solar System, and particularly on that two-bit planet that's barely visible, Earth. And why on Earth, infinitesimal as it is and provided with many other attractions, my eye zooms in on the tall girl with two purple pigtails who at every opportunity is shoving her arm up a cow's ass. The universe teems with dazzling inlets and vast panoramas, with rarefied interstellar wastes, abrupt flourishes of incandescent gases, wells of blackest void. And yet without my being aware, my gaze (let's keep calling it that) darts down to the Milky Way and homes in on the arm in the backside, and the long, bespectacled face of the giantessa performing the operation, who wears the grave expression of someone carrying out an important task, of someone praying.

The big beanpole in farmworker's overalls has her arm deep in the cow's entrails, right up to the shoulder. The bovine allows herself to be sodomized (I can't think of another term for it; *fisting* sounds pornographic) without even a sigh, being

7

a peaceful animal. Among all those I created (even before the so-called *domestication*, which is to say, slavery), cows were and are the most pacific. Many another beast would have mauled the sodomatrix or injected her with a deadly venom, or at the very least delivered a big, hind-leg kick, but the cow stands there patiently like a human waiting for the bus at the bus stop.

This is no gratuitous act of sadism, though. The big girl, poking around in the rectum, is guiding the pointed instrument forward toward the cervix. Her fingers correcting the trajectory, she directs it past the fornix and the endocervix to the uterus, where her forefinger has located a follicle nearing dehiscence (having watched this at length, I too have become an expert). Only at this point does she engage the instrument's plunger. When you are a god, you see what's taking place both inside and out, that's your fundamental prerogative.

Let me repeat, and certainly not to boast (that would be absurd for a god): the cosmos is absolutely the most unbelievable work of art imaginable, and also the most tragic, most comic, most fabled. All flaming tropical sunsets, steely seas, glittering glaciers, and mighty waterfalls are by comparison mere tawdry sketches by some amateur dauber, poor, dull landscapes. The beauties of the cosmos literally take your breath away (a purely rhetorical figure of speech for the undersigned). Not even the divine eye (let's call it that) can ever have its fill of the infinite variety of shapes and unending metamorphoses, the ever-changing choreographies that give life to its farraginous complexity. I have spent millions of years, billions, looking at the universe, and I've never had enough. And now I'm staring blankly at the Earth, its devastations and its dumps, staring at the sodomatrix biker.

The die-hard unbeliever takes another dose of semen from the portable refrigerator and snaps it into that contraption that resembles a pistol, a ruthless assassin. She pokes a hand into the behind of another cow and removes its contents. Then back in she goes, aiding and guiding the progress of the pistolette (so it's known) toward the cervix. It's obvious she has done this many times, for her gestures, though measured and precise, are somewhat mechanical. Every so often she'll peel off her surgical gloves and go roll herself a cigarette outside the barn. With each puff, she tips her purple head back slightly as she exhales the smoke, almost as if she's blowing it in my face.

Cows are made to copulate with bulls, it's all been foreseen right down to the minutest details, and instead today humans masturbate the bulls, and once they've obtained the seminal fluid, they dilute it and dilute it again to reduce the unit cost of each fertilization. Then they freeze it, like you freeze peas, or fish. Everything is *rationalized* and *optimized* (their terms) so as to get the best results and highest profits; they don't give a hoot about how yours truly has organized things. Now I am not one who has to decide everything (contrary to what you may have heard) and in fact I'm open to any and all proposals for change. Yet it irks me to think they want to systematically alter everything I've done. How would they like it if I came to their house and moved all the living-room furniture around or used the toilet brush to stir a truffle-scented béchamel? I mean, a little respect.

Even so, the heifers are fortunate. Most of the junior bulls end up in the frying pan (with that system of theirs one bull is enough to impregnate thousands of females). I'd like to see their reaction if someone organized the same method for them, if the normal sexual act were replaced by a plastic syringe to the uterus guided via anal penetration, and there was just one male to every thousand females (the remaining nine hundred ninety-nine destined for steakhood). Not to mention that out on the street you'd see mobs of children all looking familiar: thousands of half-sibs, or at best cousins. And the widows, if we may call them that, all sleeping solo.

When she's finished plunging her arm up cows' backsides, the beanpole straps the case containing her instruments onto the bag rack of her priapic twin-cylinder motorcycle, and removes the blue overalls, beneath which she's wearing her normal neo-punk biker's gear. She puts on her helmet, mounts the bike, and takes off like a *hypervelocity star* (the typical frenzy of the atheist, if I may offer a personal—call it that—opinion). Pausing at a pastry shop, she wolfs down two cream-filled cornetti and a sfogliatella without removing the helmet. Back in town, she heads for the Institute of Molecular Genetics, where she works.

Statistically speaking (I've always wanted to employ that agnostic expression, it makes me smile) the probability that my eye should come to rest on that particular girl is far less than the chances that a particular grain of sand should twice end up in the hair of the same camel-driver.* My eye could surely find many more interesting human specimens out there, with less repellent occupations. And instead my gaze falls on her, precisely as a laser beam. You'd almost think it was seeking her out. As you might imagine, my gaze is not the exclusive and monomaniacal stare of a human being, who when (s)he fixates on something (all the more when sexual hormones are involved), it's all that exists. The fulcrum of my attention is however always her. It's something in many ways incongruous that's been *happening to me* for some time (I use those words even though technically speaking it is I who make all things happen). I tell myself I must stop staring at her, and yet I stare at her. Of course it's absurd that absurd things should happen to a god; but these are the facts. I myself imagined I was immune to any sort of *aporia*, and was convinced that certain crackpot medieval theologians† were just making mountains out of molehills.

---

* The comparison might have been more apt two thousand years ago, given that freight, including illicit freight, travels by truck and air nowadays. But that's how it came to me and that's how it stays.

† Pardon my frankness, but if there is one discipline I've always considered nit-picking it is theology. Theologians reek of superiority, as if the gods (in their surreal deductions) were *them*.

THE SELF-SERVING SIDE
OF RELIGIOUS AFFLATUS

FOR TENS OF THOUSANDS of years men worshiped river spirits, fish spirits, tree spirits, stag spirits, the spirits of hares, mountains, clouds, and rain: every type of spirit apart from that of yours truly. Some raving tramps had the gift (they thought) of communicating with this mob of spirits, and so were held in the highest esteem (like rock stars and athletes today). They would leap and spin around, waving their matted hair until they lost their senses, then, eyes rolled back in their heads and foaming at the mouth, intercede for their clients (or so they thought) hoping to obtain heaps of game, cures for diseases, assistance with various everyday problems. A pathetic spectacle. And meanwhile there I was, just waiting for them to notice I existed.

And then they finally did notice. *Better late than never*, I said to myself. For a few more millennia they still had a very limited notion of my capacities: they believed I had hung the sun in the sky to light up their days and the stars to make their nights more splendid. An eternity went by before they realized that their blessed Earth is a mere speck in the Solar System, in turn a piddly little mite in the Milky Way, one negligible molecule in the vastness of the universe. Only my great patience kept me from taking serious umbrage. And to top it off, rather than finally recognizing my merits, *rendering unto Caesar that which is Caesar's* (that boy of mine, the one reputed to be my boy at any rate, had a knack for catchy sayings), now they're spreading the rumor that the universe created itself. That it sprang forth from nothing, like a mushroom: *Big Bang*, and there's your rabbit, folks.

And let us not forget the days of the votive barbecues. The intentions were excellent, don't get me wrong, but it was as if they truly believed their next-door neighbors would be pleased to get a blast of exhaust from their sacred pyres. The more smoke they made the happier they were, the more purified they felt. Sometimes they even grilled up girls and boys; it was gruesome. All these offerings of their primitive culinary arts were in my honor, or anyway in honor of my supposed colleagues (they thought of us as a flight squadron). And they were convinced we would be tickled pink (what a turn of phrase). Not to mention that they almost always left me just the offal. Filet for the gentlemen; for me, acrid exhaust fumes and bloody innards.

There are many other more recent liturgical customs that irritate me. If there's a class of buildings I never liked (for example), it's churches. I find them dark and gloomy, too tall, too truculently monumental. Depressing, macabre. Full of chilly marble, ghoulish statues, sanctimonious paintings, furnishings and symbols in bad taste. And I could never bear the smell of incense; it gives me a headache (as it were) even to think of it.

But what leaves me most baffled is the self-serving side of their religious afflatus. It's obvious that they pray because they want something in return. They bow down to me and try to get on my good side the way you would pay an insurance policy, so that you're covered whatever happens. Or worse, they think of me only when things turn really awful, the way you call the fire department in an emergency. They praise me, pay me compliments, flatter me, but in fact their only concern is to cover their asses (apologies, but that is the most appropriate term), and of course to improve their material situation. They'd like to be able to acquire larger quantities of shares and real estate, they'd like to have access to more liquidity, they imagine this will make them happier. Above all, they don't ever want to die.

It shouldn't be so difficult to understand that their lives are thrilling and tender *because* they come to an end. But no, to deny the facts, to stave off resignation, to fool themselves into thinking they'll continue to live on even after death, they invent a load of cock and bull. They dream that once they've *passed* (their term) they'll find themselves in a beautiful park supplied with chaise longues and tropical fruit trees and the luxury hotel treatment. Utter foolishness, as even a child could see. You imbeciles, other animals also kick the bucket, and you can see in their eyes (those that have eyes) that they're not bursting with joy, that it's quite a nuisance, and yet they take it well, they just lie down and wait to expire.*

Humans haven't learned how to die yet, and worse, the more time goes by, the more they think they've understood everything and the less prepared they are. It's the rare specimen who faces the advent of decomposition with a modicum of dignity and gets it over with quickly. Most abandon what little restraint they have; they pray, they suddenly remember to pray, beseeching me to put them back together if only for a few days, or if there's no hope at all, to make it easy on them. Even the ones who don't seem to be in such a bad way can rarely resist the weeping and solemn declarations and crazy vows. They're ludicrous. Sad sacks.

---

* We're talking about millions of billions of ants every year, of billions of billions of billions of microbes every second, not some piddling number. What if every insect, every single earthworm, began to moan and groan when its time came, to issue solemn declarations and beg to be granted the big pardon?

15

LAB TWO–ZERO

THE LOFTY BIKER ascends the stairs three at a time, whips through the fire door on the second floor, slips by the director's office hermetically sealed in metagenomic thoughts. She arrives in her laboratory that smells, like every laboratory in the world, of chemicals and plastic, says hello to her fellow researchers, who respond with that bleak affability typical of the disciples of genetics. Her purple-pimpled colleague, as soon as he sees her, turns the color of red-hot lava and looks like he's about to burst into tears. She raises her eyes heavenward and puts on a white coat over her post-punk uniform.

The tall one's at work on a project that aims to *create* (yes) bacterial strains that can produce alcohol from wood waste. They blast helpless microbes with scorpion and porcini mushroom genes hoping to activate an appetite for sawdust.* Her

---

* The unfortunate bacteria have lived in peace for four billion years reproducing themselves millions of times a day, thus giving birth to billions of individuals. (If some bacterium wanted to organize a Christmas dinner with his closest relatives, even supposing he could track down the names and addresses, he would have to send out billions of billions of billions

job title (adjunct technical staff) and pay rank might suggest she was hired as unskilled labor, but in fact she's so good at inventing modifications and calculating results (she's always been nuts about mathematics) that the director of the laboratory has published eminent scientific papers under his own name. Papers written by her, naturally.

Cellulose-digesting bacteria excite her only up to a point, however; she's keener on microbes that produce electricity. She wrote her PhD thesis on bacteria-powered batteries, and even won one of those scientific prizelets awarded for original ideas considered completely impracticable. And she's continuing the project on the sly, secretly putting together a network of researchers from various countries who think the idea is promising. She's convinced it's just a question of time.

Mid-afternoon, the unfailingly well-dressed lab director strides in, and uttering a tangle of phrases that hover over the void like unfinished bridges, asks the giantessa where she is with the statistical calculations they spoke of the day before. He studies the floor, his brow just slightly less unlined than usual, his perennial self-satisfied smile bobbing up to the surface like a stubborn corpse. Extracting one earbud, she replies that the results are very interesting indeed and she'll

of invitations.) If there's something that bugs me (just a figure of speech, obviously), it's that instead of going to battle with crocodiles or piranhas, creatures that can defend themselves somewhat, that lily-livered species of humans go after bacteria. One more proof, should we need another, of their cowardice.

send them right over by email. She too speaks as if she has a mild stomachache, in their usual style of communication. Or rather, their usual style since one evening six months before when they found themselves alone together because they had to complete (she did; he, for the most part, obstructed) an important trial.

He, stroking his wondrously relaxed jaw, had asked why didn't they step out on the balcony and smoke one of her hand-rolled cigarettes. She had knitted her brows slightly because the desire in his tomcat eyes looked somewhat more sexual than nicotinic (not to mention that he doesn't smoke). But hooking the distal phalange of his little finger in hers and looking him in the eye, she smiled faintly the way she does when going into sex mode. At that point his perfectly shaven and cologned face advanced on hers (although he is the shorter) and she somehow made their lips meet. She put a hand on his fly, squeezing his already erect member. After some tottering and fumbling with buttons and zippers he had tried to penetrate her by shoving her up against the big 15,000-rpm centrifuge, the way they do in the movies.

Then she sat him on the floor under the plastic beaker collecting distilled water, and mounted him the way she does her bike when she's in a rush. This for coitus number one. For number two, she knelt and he took her from behind, also on his knees (the height difference here being insignificant). This second time, too, she had no orgasm; it was 2–0, in short. Honestly, I don't like to watch some things human beings do.

But as you can imagine there's no roof nor wall nor duck blind nor sheet nor wile that stands in the way of a god; unfortunately I must put up with all of it. And then they actually did go out on the balcony of the reagent room to smoke a cigarette. He lit one too, coughing a little.

The dapper director, who's a practicing Catholic* with a wife and two daughters at home, trusts that the matter's been filed in the top-secret drawer; he's fervently counting on it. For the most part it is only at scientific conferences (which seem to serve primarily that purpose and where the risks are minimal) that he will jump a female colleague, jump her like a rooster in the henhouse. He feels pretty sure that the purple-haired girl is not the sort of nitwit who's going to preen about the thing in public or even confide in some bosom friend. In spite of the neo-metropolitan get up, her only real heartthrob is scientific research, he reckons, and from the way she fixes him with those far-apart eyes, he doesn't think she's upset with him. However, he's not one hundred percent easy about it. That mummified gentility of his, in short, is fear.

I watch the narcissist stride athletically back to his office, his behemoth of a desk perfectly clean of any clutter, and can't help but reflect that men, in their grotesque presumption, consider themselves superior and unique when instead they are

---

* It is no secret that those who pontificate and preach are the same who trespass most in the shadowy backwaters of practice; if I had to tote up all the merriment taking place in sacristies and convents over the past thousand years it would take me a decade.

clumsy and shapeless, obtuse, sex-crazed* and monomaniacal, ready to fall for every sort of superstition and fanaticism, to mutually eradicate one another and commit bestial acts that make your hair stand on end. And if that were not enough, they're infested with parasites inside and out and with terrible contagious diseases. They're dangerous, in short. Not to mention quick to putrefy.

If I were capable of second thoughts (*a priori* out of the question), the one thing I'd regret would be having created *them*. Without men, evil would not exist, nor the whole shebang of infamy and atrocities that go with it, and the cosmos would be utterly perfect. No infanticides, no blood feuds, wars, massacres of the innocents, holocausts. If I could do it again (another meaningless expression) I'd recreate the giraffes, the fleas, the walruses, the dinosaurs (poor things, came to a bad end), the salamanders, and I might even throw in some novel items, as always happens when you remake something from scratch and new ideas come to you, but one thing I wouldn't do is put man back in circulation. I'd leave Noah on the dock. *Ban the Man*, as the nuclear disarmament people would say.

---

* Merely in order to copulate, those big hairless apes lie to each other and themselves, dissimulate, cheat, squander fortunes, destroy friendships and marriages, bleed themselves dry, murder each other, all the while employing creativity and invention far beyond that applied to their technical progress. If I could begin again I'd endow them with a *libido* (a term that always reminds me of the name of a rock group) one hundred times more moderate than what they have, or limit its activity to a brief period each year, as I've done with many other species (and therefore, among other things, there would be a lot fewer of them).

Having completed what she was meant to do and also what according to the protocol she wasn't meant to do, the brainy biker now heads straight home to the former fishmonger's shop she's minimally converted into a dwelling, and once inside the door strides straight to the toilet and sits down to pee with her blind cat on her knees. She then empties a tin of rice and tuna into the cat's dish. For herself, she snaps open (dull thwack) a can of sweet corn, adds some olive oil, half a finely sliced onion, some salted capers, some white raisins, and seated on the floor in front of the television, digs in with a spoon, from time to time biting off some cheese (fontina) from the piece she holds in the other hand. Before retiring to sleep in the large green-tiled fish tank, she watches a ghastly TV show about a beautiful young woman who was supposed to marry an airplane pilot but instead dallies with his ex, a female lifeguard. First she masturbates by kneading the cushion between her legs and then using her fingers (in short, a real eyeful).

I AM PERFECT

I AM GOD and I am wrapped in silence. A silence consonant with my divine office. A silence that is also a deafening roar, a cacophony of clanging and hissing sometimes unfolding into a heavenly symphony, sometimes just one noise drowning out the other. A silence that is blinding light, a blaze of too many colors, but also perpetual darkness. I'm putting this badly, though, for as you can imagine it is not easy to describe my existence (let's call it that) in clumsy human language. The language resists, it refuses to admit my transcendence. Languages were made for (wo)man.

I am God, and I am perfect (and thus there is nothing more untrue than the expression *nobody's perfect*). My perfection is uncontestable, it is axiomatic. You might think that in the long run my utter absence of defects, even tiny ones, would grow tedious, especially when there is no great stampede to admire it (and in fact there is no one at all in the vicinity), but that isn't the case, because perfection entails having a perfect character (none of that rage and cruelty you find in the Bible) as well as an imperfectible—already free of impurity—patience. Perfection is also achieved by perfecting perfection.

Although this is the first time I've expressed myself, I do not stammer on words I've never used before, I don't stumble over complex constructions; the words well up (to employ a hydraulic metaphor) like water from a spring. I merely feel ever so slightly giddy from time to time, as when one is just beginning to fall ill. I am immense, and my immensity must pass through the lexicon's narrow neck and the obligatory pathways of syntax (resembling the twists and turns of a digestive system). It's a *sensation* (as much as that term can mean anything referring to a god) like that experienced by speleologists as they slither forward into the rocky grip of a cave.

Sometimes I ask myself, why did I create them, human beings? Let me emphasize that it didn't happen as the Bible asserts (one of the most unreliable and delusional storybooks ever written). I started creating (I no longer remember why), and all of a sudden I was peering at microbes so minute even a divine eye could scarcely make them out, huge, lumbering ruminants, tiny plants, fungi and algae, serpents, cacti, shellfish, gnats. It's not true that fish appeared and the next day, animals (the *next day?*); I created and created, and before I knew it there was a huge potpourri of animal and vegetable species. It's all very well being omniscient, but there are some things that just blow you away.*

---

* During creation one is so intent that nothing surprises (it's a sort of trance); nevertheless I invite you to imagine what it feels like to have a brontosaurus staring at you as if to work out whether he's seen you somewhere before, and what the hell he must have been up to last night not to remember diddly squat.

Certainly, as soon as I laid eyes on them I knew what each of these species was called, and how they were made, et cetera et cetera (obviously), but still, I would be lying if I said that in one precise instant I decided to create a creature called x that looked like such and such, and then another called y that looked like so and so, and so on. No, I was taking the inspiration as it came, winging it, as they say. Picasso, too, was amazed to see what came splashing forth from his brush, so you can just imagine just how volcanic my creation was, considering that I am omnipotent. This was the situation (I won't say chaotic, but confusing, yes) in which, without me having decided anything specific, man came forth. Anyone who imagines a long and meticulous drafting as an architect might do, a craftsman's patient perfecting and polishing, could not be more mistaken. What is more, that bunkum about *in His own image* is thoroughly exaggerated, although there is some slight family resemblance; I noticed it myself immediately.

THE SUPPER OF
THE CRUCIFICIAN
IMMOLATION

HUMANS ABOUND, although in comparison with bacteria (for example) they can almost be considered a species on the way to extinction. They teem in all four corners of that little planet that designates itself Earth, so that many regions seen from on high look like colonies of Enterococcus, a condition exacerbated by the pestilential fumes and lights that pollute the night. You might suppose that I watch all the geographic regions equally (divisions in nation-states make little sense to me). But no, I mostly keep an eye on what's happening in that tatty little Italian boot that (*rightly and properly*) gobbled up the Papal State in the nineteenth century. Focusing in particular on a large city in the north not very far from a mountain chain famous for its rupestrian beauties. And more in particular, on that strapping blond mademoiselle (blond when not tinted purple), half skinny (on top) and half hefty (below) and intolerably sure of herself. I myself struggle to understand why.

That afternoon, the bespectacled beanpole, skipping her sacrilegious big game hunt, goes straight home. This time she cooks rice with okra, following a recipe she invents as she goes. She also makes an algae salad with capers and pickles that smell of oyster shells and the Atlantic. When she's finished she goes to the storeroom with the bayonet window that looks out on the alley of Nigerian prostitutes, takes the door off its hinges and mounts it on two sawhorses ordinarily used to hold up complex stratigraphs of clothing. Over this she throws a colorfully striped tablecloth made from a parachute, the gift of a Swiss athlete with whom she'd had three or four two-zeros.

These preparations of hers irritate me but I can't stop watching, I observe her every move, weigh her every sigh. You could call it a *maniacal interest* if it made any sense in the case of a god to speak of interest, let alone maniacal. You could call it a *fixation*, which suits me even less. If not an *obsession*. What's certain is that nothing like this has happened to me in many billions of years; that's what floors me. I've never felt less divine.

When her two guests arrive, the lanky microbiologist reaches into a woven plastic bag under the computer station with its tangle of screens and towers and pulls out a handful of crucifixes, stacking them head to foot in a neat pyre in the tiny fireplace. She sets them alight with the help of some pages from an old microelectronics review. Even before the little pyre catches fire she warms her hands over it as if it were winter, and after a moment of hesitation so do her guests, a wee female and her good-looking male companion. It's June already, but it's still raining and summer is a long way off. For a while all three watch the flames dancing among the crucifixes without saying anything.

If she thinks she's going to shock me, she's quite mistaken. I've seen far worse: human beings burned at the stake and drawn and quartered, gruesome rapes, steaming torrents of blood, genocides. I find the fanatical geneticist a bit sad, actually—that beaky long face of hers like a highly alert bird. Her and her militant atheist accomplices. Let them rip all the crucifixes off the walls and burn them, these are certainly not the things that count. True, a father doesn't enjoy seeing images of his son (especially an only son, and deceased young) set on fire, but there's no point in making a tragedy out of it. There are hundreds of millions of crucifixes around; a dozen more, a dozen less, mean nothing. Anyway, I never much liked the pose in which the poor kid was immortalized: too bombastic, too melodramatic, too human.

Even supposing that madman really is my son. Truth is, I knew nothing about it until he burst onto the scene and began proclaiming to the four winds of Palestine that he was *the Son of God*. There have always been droves of nutcases ranting on about such things, sometimes from the top of a date palm tree. Celebrity has a price, as some pontificator said. The difference was that this one could convert a corpse, and so rather than toss him in the dungeons, they got down on their knees, copied down everything he said and didn't say, bombarded him with questions, followed him everywhere. Unbelievable. Because he really was my son, or because he was better at leading them down the garden path? I confess it's not a dilemma that keeps me awake at night.*

When the crosses are burning nicely, the lanky unbeliever adds another, larger crucifix to the fire. Only when the pyre really gets crackling does she lay on a big blue angel. Atheists think they can do away with me by despising religious froufrou. They don't realize that the more they go at it, the more they sink into the quicksand of their own faith in reverse, fall back on surrogates destined to leave them in the lurch (look what became of communism!). I'm always somewhat astonished (insofar as a god can be astonished) to think how seriously they underestimate me. Doesn't it even occur to them that I'm here watching, that I could swallow them in one bite? Maybe I should be annoyed, but instead I find them kind of sweet. Like children when you see them make some lewd gesture they don't understand.

The tall one and the wee one had met each other a few days earlier in a crowd of nutcases kissing and necking in the

---

* At first I had no doubts at all: he was a charlatan, an impostor. But then I heard so much and such various commentary that even I began to feel unsure, I who better than anyone else ought to know whether or not he's my son and how he was conceived. If there's one thing the theologians have always been good at, it's smoke and mirrors: according to some religions he existed, for others, no; for some his nature is more human than divine, for others more divine than human—in short, a tremendous muddle. So far as I'm concerned, if someone wants to believe, fine, if instead (s)he's skeptical, that's fine too; the important thing is that they believe in me. Relatives, even those who put themselves out for the cause, matter only up to a point. I hope I won't disturb anyone in stating this frankly.

middle of the road, individuals of the same sex I mean.* Now
they're babbling away beside the burning angels and crucifixes.
The tall one says that it's the church's fault that the country
still doesn't have a law protecting homosexual couples; the
church stands in the way of all progress in civil rights and
scientific research. The wee one replies that nothing's likely
to happen soon: it certainly won't be that smiley new pope
who'll upend that lethal fascist crime syndicate that's been
persecuting genuine spirituality from the beginning. The
boyfriend is studying a collection of votive phalluses atop a
bamboo chest, his brow furrowed: that is, the way men listen
to women talking to one another.

Obviously, it bothers me somewhat that these two girls
(as well as their partner in crime pretending an interest in
priapic statuettes) take it for granted I don't exist. I mean, who
wouldn't be peeved: you're there, you hear every word, you see
what's behind every single breath and syllable, and they act like
you don't exist and never have. It's not merely bad manners,
it's a question of a total lack of recognition, considering that
it is I who made the firmament and all creation (as they say).
However, if they think they can get at me by disparaging the
church, they've got the wrong man (so to speak). I've never
granted the slightest indulgence to the institution, nor to
that kid they call my son (and who probably isn't). If there's an
institution that has always caused me trouble, it's the church.

---

* Don't get me wrong, I have nothing against homosexuals, but if I created
men and women it was for some purpose, if you know what I mean.

After gazing at the crucifician immolation for some time, the three of them sit down at the table: she on the side of the fish-counter-become-kitchen-counter with the hunk sitting across from her, and the wee one next to the glass blocks that face out on the post-proletarian shop-yard. She tells them that she's worked for a number of years in a genetic research unit but also has a fallback job in bovine insemination. *So, you've got a thing for microbes?* says the hunk, in a tone that would like to sound horrified but in fact just sounds phony. *Oh yes*, says she, her face all tender. *Our future is in their hands!* she declares, like some nun in the throes of mystical abandon. To hear her raving like that sets my teeth on edge (you might say), but it would be the end of me if I had to correct every piece of balderdash humans say. I'd have to step in tens of billions of times a day.

I'M HAVING A BLAST

WHAT I LIKE BEST, when I have some time for myself (you know what I mean) is to dillydally (what a verb: I dillydally, you dillydally, they had a brief dillydalliance) around the galaxies and intergalactic spaces. I know of no spectacle more intense and thrilling than galaxies and clusters of galaxies. If I could, if I never had to toil, I would do nothing else. Keep in mind, however, that the distinction between labor and free time is meaningless for a god, because inevitably mine is not really labor, and even less so is my free time really *free*. Simplifying as much as possible, or we'll never get to the bottom of this, let us say that whenever I can I like to *putter around.**

Let me be clear: when I move through the universe I do not strut about like the owner of a great corporation in the hallways of his headquarters, and even less like a scowling

---

* Perhaps I should say *zoom around*, given the velocities infinitely greater than the speed of light (never mind quantum physics). If I prefer *putter*, it's precisely to emphasize the completely relaxed and soothing nature of my activity. As always, I must explain myself in broad approximations.

Tolstoyan latifundista on horseback. The term that comes closest, although it's still profoundly inadequate, is *tourist*. Like a tourist, I have no precise objective, like a tourist my frame of mind is receptive and benevolent, I'm unstressed, I like to compare, digress. Of course I know that tourism is widely considered anything but a spiritual activity, but in my view, if all tourists acted like tourists in their everyday lives too, the so-called world would be a lot better off.

There are dozens of billions of galaxies, and even the paltriest of them has tens of millions of stars of all colors, stars with halos in various styles, pretentious plumes, nebulae in the most garish colors, even planets and satellites. Some stars are as quiet as little angels despite the deadly nuclear reactions inside them; most however seem to be possessed by the devil, hawking up foaming lava that swells into giant bubbles, or just the opposite, collapsing and shriveling until they nearly disappear, a billion times denser than lead. But the interstellar spaces, too, with their fresh and invigorating atmosphere measuring two hundred sixty degrees below zero (to use a scale everyone can understand) and their glimmers of all but impalpable dust, are by no means wastelands without any appeal, and they vary greatly. In short, it's almost impossible to get bored.

There's such a quantity of stars, each one putting on a fabulous show, that every galaxy is a sort of multiplex with millions or billions of screens. And so you could not altogether mistakenly characterize my existence as having season tickets to a billion multiplexes with millions of billions of screens.

I watch all the films at once, however, and they are shown (as it were) 24/7. It's not so different from the job of control-room supervisor of a megagalactic nuclear power plant; my locus, my *workstation* (shall I call it that?), is something like a cyclopean control room.

You might object that I've already seen what I'm about to see, and thus it's not that much fun. But that would be quite misleading. As if a tram conductor who had worked in a particular city for millions of years could remember the faces of all his passengers, how they were dressed, what stop they got off, et cetera et cetera. With my limitless powers, I have no problem at all picturing each of the billions and billions of stars in detail, but when I find myself there looking I'm forever amazed by all the variety—I get caught up and, moral of the story if I may use a somewhat profane expression, I find I'm *having a blast*.

One big difference with the movies are the smells. That's one of the greatest appeals. At times the scents are delicate, suggesting vanilla, or cinnamon, or there will be a faint smoky smell, like a cigarette perceived from afar, or better, a pipe. More often there are violent fumes of ether or acetone, or polycyclic aromatic hydrocarbon vapors or other deadly organic compounds that bring to mind the crater of an angry volcano or some industrial park full of chemical plants. Stinks and stenches don't bother me at all (whatever those bigoted theologians may say), they make me think of the fierce violence of certain magnificent expressionist paintings. I'm certainly no fop who lives on rose water and the smell of soap; at times

I greedily fill my lungs (so to speak) with acrid fumes, or even just nitrous oxide, which makes me laugh until the tears come. Just as the dung-scented aroma of Kolkata has nothing to do with Copenhagen's coniferous tang, I can recognize many a galaxy by its smell alone.

MOONMILK

WHEN THEY FINISH the algae and capers with a dash of mountain larch lichen essence, the beanpole asks Don Giovanni what he does with himself. With a deep sigh of false modesty, Vittorio (no loser's name for him) replies he is studying pointless stuff. For example? For example, moonmilk. In a somewhat breathy voice she says she didn't know that moons produced milk, and he says not all do, but some, yes. *And how do you milk them?* she asks, her bird eyes widening like a child's. Moonmilk, he tells her, is a limestone secretion found in caves, you just go there with a suitable container and collect the stuff. *And then you drink it?* It sounds as if she's swallowing a big stone. Pushing back a wayward neoromantic lock, he replies that in fact moonmilk serves to quantify man-made environmental damage, in other words to certify our probable cause of death.

There in the former fishmongers' shop, you see, an ancient ritual is being played out. Men talk, their words a screen to conceal their basest instincts. The fact is, the fetching young man has the hots for the bacteria manipulator and cow inseminatrix. You don't have to be the supreme being to notice: his pupils are as big as marbles and every word that comes out of his throat sounds like a caress. His girlfriend can see it; she's got her sights locked on the scoundrel, once again up to his tricks. The godless microbiologist, however, is *playing dumb*. She gets up to put another crucifix on the fire, which is now a bit sluggish, and with a long-handled fork pushes all the crossless redeemers to one side. Poor half-smoked devils, they make a noise like a rusty old chain. They might be soldiers with their arms flung out at the moment of death—or maybe they're already deceased, thus the rigor mortis appearance.

The lanky unbeliever, whose upper half resembles a skinny, asymmetric El Greco figure, her lower half a plump young Titianesque matron (I've always been an art lover, ever since the first cave paintings) sits down again, this time with her chair facing the IT guerrilla workstation and her elbows resting on the chair back. In a dopey female voice, she says she'd love to taste moonmilk. *Frailty, thy name is woman!* The devious male, an amiable smile on his face, says that nothing could be simpler: if she likes he'll take her to a cave that's full of it. Rivers of lovely milk.

There are times when I think that it's not all that wonderful to know in advance how everything will turn out. I wouldn't mind watching my film from start to finish, noshing on popcorn in peace (I've always been drawn to that greasy, earthy smell).* As I was saying, the problem with being God is that you see what humans don't. I'm no prophet, but I can see the future a million times better than any old soothsayer or

* Before I began to *think*, everything was okay with me. I would never have dreamed of finding even an infinitesimal reason to complain. But now, I see, my words reveal many dissatisfactions, many unattainable desires.

fortune-teller. Not only that, I can see the past. For example, I'm aware that one evening the previous week, our dreamboat told his wee mate he was going to the gym and instead he went straight over to see her best friend. They fell into bed almost immediately, and he came twice and she once. Then late at night he returned to sleep at his mother's house. Good Italian son that he is, he's still tied to mamma's apron strings.

So maybe we could all go on an outing to the cave together? The fierce atheist is in an ecumenical mood. The tiny one, shoulders quivering like a tender fawn, says that caves give her claustrophobia. She'd gone in one once but felt like she was back in prison, and nearly suffocated. Thinking that she'd been rude to their host, she is now trying to compensate. (A reader may wonder how the writer knows what a character's thinking, but in my case the point's moot.) Don G., in a typical petty male reaction, takes his girlfriend literally, and remarks that she much prefers an iguana to a cave, that's the problem. *We're all free to find iguanas more interesting than holes in a mountainside*, she replies, revealing her gum-colored gums. *At least my caves don't bite*, he shoots back, showing off a scar on the side of his hand.*

---

* If there is one sphere in which humans reveal their lack of perfection, it's *the couple*. I personally have never seen a pair of penguins shouting vile accusations at each other about mothers-in-law or nail scissors. Humans on the other hand are forever dissatisfied, they seem to go out of their way to find reasons to squabble. Or rather, after a brief pacific idyll comes a crescendo of misunderstanding and reciprocal intolerance until full-scale war breaks out. Not a pretty picture in a species so devoted to crooning love tunes, one that considers itself a thousand times superior to all others.

After she pours them coffee with cardamom pods, the lanky microbiologist throws two hefty blocks of wood on the fire. The spelunker, testosterone thrumming, wonders if the logs came from a crucifix, and she says they were beams swiped from a nearby building site, next to the Indian who sells cell phones supplied by the Camorra. She answers as though she regrets no crucifix was involved.

Now the iguana-lover speaks up, her voice as pure as a jet of water, languidly caressing the words. Has she always burned crucifixes? Oh boy, I knew the reptile-hugger would soon come to hate her tall rival—hate her with every neuron of her brain, every cell of her myocardium—but right now you might almost think she likes her. Rosa Luxemburg of the purple locks replies that she's been burning them for years, only when it's cold, of course. *If everyone did, it would solve the problem of the Catholic Church's overweening power*, says the seducer, currying favor. His wee friend asks where she found all those crucifixes and the other looks blank as though she doesn't understand the question. *Nailed to the wall*, she says finally, seeing no polemical intent, just plain curiosity.

HUMANS,
THEIR PREPOSTEROUS CONCEIT

A GOOD MANY human beings believe God's at their service. Billions of them, even the most dismal failures, the least presentable, bask in the ludicrous conviction that God has nothing better to do than indulge their petty, insignificant point of view, see the universe from their perspective. Which, you understand, would be technically possible: the ability to perform multiple tasks, to identify with an infinite number of subjects—to seven billion human beings we must add billions of billions of billions of protozoa, insects, arachnids, myriapods, sponges, annelids, mollusks, springtails, and so forth and so on—the exponential multiplication of points of view, that is, and the filing of all the necessary information, are just some of the basic tricks of the trade.

So I repeat, it would be doable. But I don't do it. A god must keep his distance, if only to maintain his image and avoid spreading himself too thin. But also to allow each of them to show what he or she is worth morally. It would be pointless to set up the Last Judgment (supposing I were in fact to realize that tribunal my alleged son is always going on about—in short, to calculate the bottom line). My *philosophy*, to use a word I've never liked, is this: *Grant everyone the maximum freedom, then do the accounting.*

Others—many, too many—make the opposite mistake. They are convinced I don't exist. These are the fundamentalists of reason, science, and progress, the fanatics of logic, of the French Revolution, social leveling and democratic procedure. The type who go around saying God is just a drug, that minus God human beings could finally realize themselves and be content (as if anything would satisfy them for long). Emaciated philosophers and poets who grin nervously, swelling with pride to think they can face existence without a shred of meaning or sense. And above all, billions of wise guys who take advantage of my absence to wallow in materialism, with no thought for anything but consuming as many goods as possible, pleasuring themselves to the max day after day. In place of the old rites (but in need of some liturgical celebration) they mount noisy musical performances and ball games, these too steeped in commodity fetishism.

And then there are the in-betweens, the chronically undecided. The way they see it, maybe I exist and maybe not, maybe I've got the cosmos in hand and maybe I don't, maybe I'm omnipotent and maybe I'm a figment of some-body's imagination, like Sancho Panza and Emma Bovary: they don't know and they can't be bothered to find out. They shrug their shoulders, they're proud to be so open-minded. Quite often these opportunists dabble in certain fanciful religions that hold I'm an Immense Intelligence, a Supreme Postulate, a Cosmic Essence, the Big Poo-Bah. In some ways these maxi-vacillators are even more of a pain in the backside than the infidels, if I may say so. I wouldn't mind suddenly materializing before them wearing my big beard, hair receding at the temples (according to the painters of the Renaissance and the Baroque), to see how they react. *Somebody looking for me?* I'd snarl, like the Most Wanted dude in a crime movie. *Anybody want a kick where the sun don't shine from the Universal Hive Mind?*

Of course it's not easy for a human being to understand who I am, how I think (as it were), what I'm capable of. It's like asking a protozoan to describe an elephant: he could tell you about an infinitesimal portion of one hair on the scrotum, or about a single epidermal cell from the auditory canal of the right ear, in short whatever was right there before him, but he'd never be able to describe the elephant in all its majestic entirety. Obviously the difference between (wo)man and me is a billion billion times greater than that between a human and a protozoan, and an elephant does not embody the meaning of all things; mine was just a rather vivid example.

If you want to gauge how discerning they are, just look at how well they understand one another. From scraps of information, misunderstandings and misinterpretations, they stitch up a crazy quilt of inferences, enhancing the picture with bits of their own unrelated experience, void of logic, far from the facts, often quite contradictory and even perfectly antithetical. Wrapped up in this Harlequin's coat they spin mad plots and fairy-tale fantasies that explain little more than their own obsessions and failures.

And yet, most things (wo)men do are peculiarly in accord with the way they'd like to be seen. They spend most of their time misleading, pretending, feigning, and dissimulating. Truth is, every human being is a shrewd professional liar, a seasoned actor capable of great performances. Faking it is one of their native talents—also necessary and characteristic—just as nightingales are born to sing and kangaroos to hop. Every species has a specialty; theirs is charlatanism. In short, they were created defective, and things have only gone downhill with time. My self-appointed son, I mean the emaciated hippie who claims he came forth from third-party insemination, tried to sort them out, but he seems to have done more harm than good. ·

I have to admit, though, at times they're entertaining. Not that a god needs amusement, God forbid, but these clowns are so full of themselves, they're such hucksters, so reliably unpredictable, immoral, and nuts that anyone observing them is soon transfixed. They're devious, like television: you end up glued to the screen even if you're not interested, even when you know it's just an indiscriminate ploy to grab your attention. Lucky for them they have no competition. There's not a single form of organic matter in the entire universe that even faintly matches their sly industriousness, ubiquitous meddling, clumsy-but-cunning illogic, their skill at getting something out of every new situation.

SO-CALLED LOVE IN GESTATION

THE FOLLOWING DAY the giantessa with the sideways braidlets wakes in a good humor. As dawn breaks under the raised awning, she waves good morning to the Indian across the street, who's now busy converting his bedroom into a shop. Outside, mounting her twin-cylinder, she takes off. At the Cattle Breeders Federation she selects, from the vials nested in liquid nitrogen, doses of the semen of a German bull that's all the rage that season. Then she's off for another Alpine valley not far from the city but not wrongly considered quite backward.

The owner of the dairy farm is a typical denizen of this valley of pre-digital cavemen, and with a cigarette clenched between his teeth, his muttering is hard to understand. She removes her helmet and he can't believe his eyes: not only is her hair purple, she's not a man. An artificial inseminator who's female, wears a ring in one nostril and a black leather jacket with studs is quite a novelty. Paralyzed, he hovers next to her throughout the entire operation, eyes bulging at her every move, ready to let out a scream. As she always does in these situations, she pretends not to notice. From time to time she has to cope with one of these lobotomized farmers. She doesn't treat the matter lightly, though; she knows she must perform better than the best male around if she wants to be judged his equal. She can feel the yokel's tribal gaze burning into her hands and skin. If he had the nerve he'd confess his doubts, the way you complain to a trusted friend. She's had that happen too.

Our tall sorceress doesn't wonder why she's so cool about this oaf literally breathing down her neck, she doesn't ask herself why she's feeling euphoric. She's distracting herself using a tried and true human technique, thinking about the night before. Not about Prince Charming's ravishing good looks, but about his girlfriend. That medieval peasant outfit she had on was lovely, and she looked good in it, she has a natural elegance. The giantessa doesn't usually go for the thrift-shop look, it reminds her of old photos of her mother. But this sticks in her mind. You don't have to be a mind reader, though, to know that pretty soon, she and the fellow with the hieratic hairstyle—drawn together by their mutual Darwinian fundamentalism—will gang up and eliminate her rival. Not that they'll necessarily be an item for long, mind you.

Humans, rather than simply mate and be done with it like other animals, make a huge drama of so-called love. They suffer and sigh, they get all sentimental, become inebriated in a sea of noble aspirations, make crazy promises. We're not yet at that stage here, however, for right now our young microbiologist is merely lost in contemplation of moonmilk and the risks of climate change. In any case, she's a novice;

up to now, her *love stories* (I adhere to the formulation) have been limited to a single copulative contact, sometimes two or three and very rarely four or five. These trial sessions tend to establish that the male in question isn't her type. The scores say it all: two–zero, one–zero, three–zero. Forever zero, home game or away. Undiscouraged, she fishes out, more often now online, still another individual with XY chromosomes, but things won't go well there either: one–zero, three–zero, two–zero. And no particular empathy.

It's been like this since she was fourteen, when in order to have sex she had to sneak out of her fundamentalist boarding school like a cat in heat. Even to her the thing is starting to seem a bit peculiar, but she's not disheartened, she's an optimist, a real Sagittarius (in case you were wondering whether I have anything against the zodiac—I don't). People who know her consider her a free spirit, but freedom has little to do with it: she's looking for the right person, and so far she hasn't nailed it. But she's convinced that sooner or later she'll succeed; it's like those scientific breakthroughs that take years to mature but then turn out to be genuine revolutions.

The Alpine Brown's rectum is narrower and shorter than that of larger breeds, and she has to squeeze her fist tight when she approaches the stretch next to the cervix. The vagina, too, is smaller and shorter. She likes Alpine Browns because they remind her of undemanding people, people who don't put on airs, but also because their contained dimensions are *heaven-sent* (sic) for her hands and arm. While she's more at ease in the job than usual, there are annoying gasps and sighs coming

45

from the nearby hominid, whose shoulders seem to be held up by an invisible coat hanger. It's obvious her moves don't convince him; he thinks she's too limp-wristed, too indecisive. She wouldn't mind telling him that an arm in the ass is an arm in the ass; cows are God's creatures too.

The dairyman huffs and puffs, he moves his legs up and down like a bear tied to a stake, he wishes she would hurry up. She's watched men do this, she'd like to say—they just want to get their right arm to the uterus and plunge the syringe as fast as possible. It's that same haste you find during sex with them, and the reason she doesn't get to orgasm. She's not wasting time, just avoiding brusque movements, getting the animal to relax. She doesn't force them.*

Removing the dark blue overalls (same color as her eyes), the tall one is thinking that maybe the farmers in some of these tribal areas would benefit from genetic improvement along with their cows. Yes, it would surely be best to begin with them. This fellow could be enhanced with a genotype that promoted an intelligent gaze, good posture and a clear voice (not this grunting like a walrus with a cigarette stuck in the corner of its mouth). Certainly, a physical specimen more in tune with the times.

---

* Human beings are adept at finding ways to soothe their consciences, and especially the human beings of that down-at-the-heel boot known as Italy. Italian thieves believe they are the most honest of criminals, the assassins fancy themselves highly altruistic; everyone has a system to balance his or her personal accounts. We'll see whether that same indulgence is applied in the court of Last Judgment.

THE POETRY OF MATHEMATICS

THE BESPECTACLED GENETICIST, all bones and pointy asymmetric angles above and maybe a little too plump below, is convinced that science can explain everything. How the universe was formed, where it's going from here, the meaning of everything that happens. In her mind, there is just one true explanation, one single transcendent entity, and that is the Theory of Evolution. She believes that one day very soon science will reveal how *life itself* came forth. Peering into her test tubes with those far-apart bird eyes, she dreams she sees the first spark of the reenactment. You'd think it was some heirloom recipe: one good solid or gaseous ingredient, a defined sequence of chemical reactions, and poof, there you have it, a living being.

She's not the only one, heaven knows. As time goes by human beings grow more and more inebriated by what they think is their unique talent: their so-called reason. They don't see that whether it's rational or irrational, cerebral activity is always faulty and misleading. Reasoning, by definition, gradually homes in on one particular aspect, revealing, in that foolish arbitrary focus, how fallacious and worthless it is. While the only truth is All, the whole, that is to say, God, the undersigned. And so-called reason is only an illusion—slightly less fickle perhaps but still utterly fanciful—of unreason, of the hardwired need human beings have to believe in something. But this they cannot know because they are unable to *think about thought* (human language makes it impossible to say that better).

Humans throw themselves into their tiny scientific breakthroughs to distract themselves from their finite condition, the way elderly women sew cross-stitch patterns on table linen to keep the aches and the pains and the approaching end at bay. And yes, they have achieved some modest results: for example, they can photograph bacteria, exchange kidneys, fly from one part of the planet to another, even if painfully slowly (the vapor trails their vehicles leave in the sky remind me of snail slime). But in order to arrive at those tiny conquests, they have wrought devastation everywhere, and put their future in question. And at every step of their so-called progress they conceal the consequences, the looming catastrophe.

It was obvious to me from the days when they began to employ their rudimentary telescopes and their Torricelli tubes that, just as the investigators of the Inquisition had perfectly understood, the aim of these *scientists* (their term) was to compete with me. So that one day they could take my place. If however these wise guys considered that a nuclear-powered rocket would take thousands of human lifetimes to cross a small-to-medium-size galaxy—not to mention clusters of galaxies—and that the temperature inside the most peaceable of stars is a couple million degrees above that of the water in which they boil their pasta, the pressure several million times greater than the cooker they use for artichokes, not to mention the fact that Andromeda is heading straight toward them at a speed of 430,000 miles per hour, well, they might be less cocky. Instead they're convinced they are advancing by leaps and bounds, that the future holds amazing promise.

And yet, and yet. I must confess that scientific discoveries have always intrigued me. Does that seem strange? Well, I never claimed to be consistent. I enjoy watching matter and organisms be ground up and digested by human intelligence (however limited), seeing complex phenomena reduced to austere algebraic formulae, to gelid equations. As you can probably imagine, the various scientific disciplines with their high-sounding names offer me no novel discoveries—given that everything was created by me *with my own hands*, I'd be tempted to say if I didn't mind sounding bombastic. I know full well what they are and what they contain, but still, I find them amusing. Paradoxically, I find that scientific *laws*, so awkward and insistently insecure, almost always have a graceful side. But above all it's the enigmatic poetry of mathematics (which for me is just a vague approximation, a baby's confused babbling) that I like.

Incongruous as it may seem, a god likes to keep up with his times, he's interested in what's new. You might even say the new *galvanizes* him, if the term, which makes me think of frogs' legs twitching, weren't so impossibly un-divine. There is really nothing new for a god; nope, it's all as ancient as the beginning of time, given that past and future are one. Still, those human novelties stir him to stay informed. To review various notions that have grown a bit vague. It's like opening at any random page a great encyclopedia written a long time ago. Anyway, I've always been curious, although that adjective needs to be purified of all its human sludge.

When I was young (allow me) I was crazy about animals; I could study them for years, for centuries. *Damn, I'm great*, I would think, impressed by how many I'd made and how different each was from another, with the strangest of habits and the most unimaginable particulars. And of course they'd change over time. They'd *evolve*, as the biologists say: these people see evolution in a pot of pasta cooking. Sure, it was all prescribed from the beginning, but there were undeniable *coups de théâtre*: fish that stood up and walked on dry land, big lizards that sprouted wings and began to fly, all kinds of stuff. I didn't need that Darwin fellow with the chronic depression to point it out to me.

As I grow older, though (as it were), I have to say it's the humans who interest me most. They bug me, that barbarous cult of technology of theirs and their contempt for the things that matter; they enrage me; I'm always thinking I must teach them the lesson they deserve. But I can't stop looking at them. I have no idea what's happening to me; it's like a drug. (A god on drugs!)

A PALEOBEATNIK'S
TRANSCENDENTAL SILENCES

ON HER WAY to work, the neo-Mendelian cow-sodomatrix stops to polish off a couple of cannoli. For the record: one, then another, then yet another (!); the Palestinian counterman's gaze ricochets up and down, to her scrawny upper body, then to her plump lower half, in search of an explanation. Restraint, she finds, is hard to achieve when it comes to sex and Sicilian cannoli. When she arrives at her little corner of laboratory, it's already almost noon and she's somewhat uneasy. Everyone knows her scientific productivity is outstanding, but she never feels she's accomplished anything. At this point one might mention the Judeo-Christian et cetera guilt complex, but it won't be me to do it, God forbid.

That afternoon she can't keep her mind on gene amplification. When she stopped for the cannoli, she had glanced at the newspaper and seen the new data on CO_2 emissions. Golden boy is absolutely right, she thinks, the politicians, rather than heed the urgent warnings of climate science, are doing their best to stoke so-called economic growth, i.e. increase pollution and set up a huge own goal. The only way out is for science to find immediate, effective responses to energy and contamination problems. People had better get on it fast. Her bacteria-fueled battery, if she can get it working, will be a contribution.

Now it bothers me a little (maybe even that's saying too much) that this girl, who's in some ways insufferable despite her many sympathetic qualities,* still doesn't realize she's been hypnotized by the paleoclimatic Casanova. I'm tempted to warn her (and yes, I can find a way, I assure you). However, I very rarely interfere in such matters. I mean, I'm no Aphrodite or Cupid, I'm a proper monotheistic deity with all that implies in terms of status and decorum. I'd never have a moment's peace if I got mixed up in such chicanery; they'd all come begging and promising me this or that for some petty sentimental or sexual favor. Whatever happens I must safeguard my transcendental dignity.

Exiting the laboratory, Ms. Einstein zigzags across town on her bike, zipping in and out of the lanes of traffic with infidel bravado. Another quick voluptuary stop—two cream filled cornetti—and she's on her way toward the hills to the south. The hideously overbuilt plain behind her, she coasts over gentle dales pocked with neo-oligarchic villas, heads down

---

* I'm the first to admit I'm amazed, because at the beginning I didn't notice these at all. However, you would be very much mistaken to think divine justice implies an unshakable, irrevocable verdict; to be just also means to evaluate elements previously overlooked, as happens in criminal justice when new evidence emerges.

the narrow valley inhabited by the dropouts, you might even say *the wasted*. When she gets there she parks her bike by her mother's friend's house (house: a euphemism). He's in the shed next to the chicken coop, head deep in the engine of a decrepit Caterpillar tractor. His orange overalls are stained with oil, and his sparse hair, beginning at the sides of his head and at the nape of his neck, is gathered into a long, scant ponytail. After she has thoroughly cuddled the two big dogs and the small one, the sex maniac—the dogs make a big fuss when she comes and squabble for *pole position*—she approaches him and makes a pecking gesture with her long bird's neck. Then her purple locks, too, disappear into the Neolithic engine.

Before a word has been exchanged, she's understood that once again the problem is the diesel pump. The only good solution would be to go out and buy a new one. Instead, they try to revive it. As always, they work in silence, apart from "pass me this" and "pass me that." Often they're engaged, as now, in antiquarian mechanics, but it could also be the rebuilding of a collapsed wall, the replacement of a bent gutter, the pruning of a comatose apple tree, and other such bucolic operations linked to a lifestyle of semimystical autarchy. She helps him, and sometimes takes over where the problem is electronic (not this tractor) or even just involving very tiny screws. Often they lack the right equipment, but usually they find a solution. Much of their pleasure derives from that.

Once they've reassembled the pump the weary tractor starts up, expelling a plume of thoroughly unecological black smoke. Pleased with their success, he passes her a filthy rag to clean her hands, and, cigarette sinking into his large Indian beard, wipes his own on an old pair of underpants. They then go inside the wood-built part of the construction—to call it a construction is perhaps to exaggerate—that serves as kitchen and living room,* followed by the two big dogs, one with a long coat, one shorthaired, as well as the small addled dog and a cat of many colors. He offers her a beer, then settles into a yoga position to roll himself a joint, the laborer at last permitting himself a well-earned reward after a hard day's work. She sits on the broken-down armchair and there they remain facing each other, not exchanging a word.

Under the porthole that gives onto the chicken coop (home to one lame and mangy duck) there's an altar decorated with a string of colored lights like the ones you hang on a Christmas tree. Below the statue of a fat man bared to the waist sits an offering of overripe bananas and a pear in the final stages of putrefaction surrounded by a halo of happy, buzzing fruit flies. *Thank heavens that slimy mess isn't addressed to me*, I say to myself. After years of ingesting psychedelics, her mother's friend is now the follower of an orientalist-leaning cult. Brain fried by long sessions of transcendental meditation, he's convinced that his lady friend has been reborn in India. Or rather, in his delirium she was first a red and yellow butterfly, and now (soul transposed with the ease with which you might move into a

---

* The original camper (back in the days of Ms. Einstein's mother, there had only been that) had been absorbed into an eclectic heap of discarded materials, like a small fish trapped in the stomach of a bigger one.

more comfortable apartment) she's a woman with a red dot in the middle of her forehead. He has no doubts whatsoever, and even claims he sees her from time to time. It's precisely to avoid listening to this lunacy that Ms. Einstein would rather not talk (and who could disagree with her?) but just sip her beer in silence.

As twilight fades to night he smokes another joint and she drinks a second beer and devotes her attention to the addled canine sex maniac, to whom she's very partial. The animals each have their own seat on some chair or cushion, for this place belongs to them above all. They're a bit puzzled, though, that food-wise nothing is happening, and seized by that restlessness that precedes a meal. *Why aren't these two amiable bipeds preparing something for us to chow down?* they wonder (I can also read animal thoughts). *Why aren't they talking to each other the way humans do?* When it's pitch dark, she shakes her purple braids and bids goodbye to that derelict creature she calls father. A man who pays the rent by watering the garden and cleaning the pool for the ex-Communist wholesaler of organic bananas.

Mounting her bike now, she heads back into town.

THE NIGHT OF THE HORNY TOADS

THE FOLLOWING SATURDAY around noon Casanova tele-phones the beanpole and, sounding distracted, proposes they meet for a drink that evening. She says she'd like that very much but she already has plans to meet up with his companion to save the besotted toads. The wind whistles right out of his sails; it seems that his wee friend has already contacted this girl (who's been monopolizing his brain for three days) and co-opted her in that horny toad soap opera. He hadn't expected a move of this kind. To gain time, he clears his throat and stammers out something unintelligible. Had his girlfriend divined something and deliberately tried to cross him? It doesn't seem very likely, but he can't dismiss that hypothesis. He's struggling to regain his cocksure good cheer, and ends up telling her he'll come along too; he's crazy about anurous amphibians.

The beanpole shows up on her motorbike at the dirt lot where they've arranged to meet. It's pitch dark and many toad-saviors are already milling around, each with a light beam projecting from their heads. The iguana-lover, she too wearing a miner's helmet, explains why they've assembled: every year at this time the toads descend from the woods toward the lake on their ancestral path to reproduction, and come smack up against a road cutting across their way. It's not even a heavily trafficked road, yet every time a ruthless toad-slaughter takes place. Until the corrupt politicians get their act together and build some tunnels under the asphalt, the only solution is to flag down the cars and give the toads a hand.

The lofty geneticist really likes the tiny zoologist's joyous energy, her calm dedication (playful, weightless, and unpredictable as a leaf in the wind). It's clear that she's absolutely at ease here—with that delicious woodsy smell, the darkness swarming with animals and nocturnal insects—it's her natural habitat, you might say. And from what she can see, all these people here look quite pleasant, people accustomed to doing good deeds. It occurs to her that maybe her lab isn't the greatest place in the world, with those emaciated, semi-depressed colleagues. She's used to electronic interactions, not encounters with bodies that exude all sorts of scents, and gentle exhalations that lightly brush a person's cheek.

At some point Don Giovanni himself materializes out of the darkness and gives her a hug, eyes down in a pretense of shyness. In truth, he's worried that in this pitch-black atmosphere his nonchalant charms may not be as effective as in a well-lit café with comfortable seating. And maybe a little concerned that this peculiar young lady may blab to his girlfriend about his phone call: a worry that makes her vaguely shadowy air seem even more mysterious and fascinating.

Meanwhile, she's so taken by this throng of affable militants that she completely forgot he was coming. To make up for it, she returns his embrace a little too energetically.

They take up their positions along the paved road and, her genetic acumen at work, our brainy scientist immediately notes that the wave of toads is in no way trying to dodge the cars. Programmed hundreds of millions of years before the first automobile, they're instead mesmerized by the headlights, probably thinking they see pairs of giant fireflies preparing to mate.*

Decked out with a lamp on her brow and a vest with reflector strips, she lends the others a hand, collecting the toads and stacking them neatly in the bucket she's been handed. When it's nearly full she gently empties it on the valley side of the road. Frequently, though, the dimwit drivers don't understand, or pretend not to understand, and refuse to be guided zigzag down the road to avoid hitting those *nasty little varmints* (everyone's free to have an opinion, God above all). Due to a pileup of the pulped brutes, stretches of the asphalt are spread with a layer of slippery mucilage, and the cars are skidding and sliding as if on ice.

But the tiny iguana-hugger has taken stock of the problem, and now seizes control of the situation. They will need to organize an alternating one-way traffic plan, she persuades

---

*   As usual I'm presenting what I know for a fact as merely hypothetical, the way writers do to avoid looking too sure of themselves. Not a very brilliant solution, but it's what they teach in "creative writing."

the others. The two volunteers at either end of the descent must keep in phone contact, and those in between will quickly remove the toads from the road surface. Along the stretch bordered by a high wall, where most of the beasts are being mauled (their saviors screaming bloody murder), she makes the drivers slow to a crawl. She knows how to deliver an order and can be brusque when necessary, but they all obey her happily because her voice is clear as a bell and utterly free of authoritarian animus. Although—but perhaps this is just my impression—she's ever so slightly whiny, à la Mother Teresa of Calcutta.

The lanky one's up at the top of the critical stretch of road and she's happy, certain to be doing something genuinely useful. She likes taking the toads in hand and placing them on the valley side, likes running to rescue the suicidal ones, likes clapping her hands triumphantly to speed the laggards along. Her long and not unfleshy legs sprint from one side of the road to the other, she bellows at the weary amphibians, terrorizes the drivers going too fast, stands in the middle of the road to make them slow down. Don Giovanni is posted near her, his face all crumpled up; he handles the toads as if they were dog droppings. Privately (I can tell you with no fear I'm mistaken) he thinks these creatures have survived long enough and it would be no tragedy if they became extinct. But he means to stay by her side and he's carrying out the mission, not without a stream of witticisms: he imitates toad calls, makes toad speeches, sings arias in toad voices. She laughs. Great mathematical skills do not a sagacious person make.

As always I can't stop staring at the damn girl: I watch her as she takes the toads into her long hands as if they were fluffy kittens, I watch her warm to the hunk, not giving him much rope but feeding as necessary his testosteronic *amour propre*. I imagine — although the verb *imagine* doesn't begin to convey in what detail I see the scene—the coitus that's coming. A three-three, I'm sure of it (I know, that's not an appropriate expression for a divinity, but it fits). I try to *think of something else*, to remove myself from the situation. But I can't take my eyes off her. I see her, and above all, I see what happens next.

Were I a little less tolerant and magnanimous, more like what those hoary old scriveners depict in the Old Testament, I'd have her struck by a passing automobile, fall backward to hit her head hard against the pavement, whack! a tiny trickle of blood, and the problem would be resolved. *Race to Hospital to Save Animal-Rights Volunteer in Vain*, the local papers would report. *The young woman was deceased before reaching the emergency room*. Finally, I'd detach my gaze from the Earth (there's only a thin film of real earth down there) and for a while I'd direct my attention to stars and galaxies. You can *thank your lucky stars* I'm nothing like the cruel God of the Book of Job, or she'd be done for.

SALVING ECOLOGIST
CONSCIENCES

THEORY OF EVOLUTION or no theory of evolution, human
beings take it for granted that I hold them above other animals,
that I consider them superior. When in fact for me, whether
they are humans, walruses, or sardines makes not a whit of
difference. When a man takes a dive I certainly don't grieve
more than when, shall we say, a microbe or a turnip bites the
dust. To tell the truth, in many ways I prefer turnips; at least
they remain silent and like many other cruciferous greens
have a genuine vegetable dignity. Not to mention the large
marine mammals, to which I'm deeply attached. How could
anyone imagine I would prefer the lowest of humans to a nice
walrus? That's just crazy.

Every day (wo)men pursue the relentless genocide of animal
and vegetable species they've been carrying out for some time
now, every day they trample a bit more of what they call their
environment (as if it had been made for them!), every day they
use their cunning, I wouldn't call it intelligence, to scrape the
bottom of the barrel of *resources*, with the idea that anything

that comes in handy has been reserved for their exclusive use. By now their frenzy has become fury; they are literally destroying the wee planet to which they're attached by gravity. Unlike bacterial colonies that proceed in silent dignity toward death, drowning in their own excrement, humans do everything they can to make sure the end will come in the most chaotic, horrific way possible.

What's especially chilling about them is their dogged and fanatical materialism. They direct all their mental and physical energies (not insignificant despite their mediocre longevity) to squandering and dissipating everything under the sun, unable to rest until they've consummated their part of the damage. The only thing they can agree on is the need to provoke as many catastrophes as possible. Unlike, for example, ants and bees and other social species, they've never shown much solidarity, and every year less. I'm no hard-line conservative, mind you, but I see no reason to wreck and demolish everything.

Most of the so-called environmentalists—and this is something I want to emphasize—are even worse: they not only think they are superior to the animals, but better than their species-mates who mistreat so-called nature. They're convinced that their speeches and spiels help save the globe from catastrophe, that they themselves are doers of good. They too profit from the coming dilapidation of all things, they too live like nabobs while passing their time lecturing everyone else. They seem to think humanity can keep up a five-star hotel lifestyle without causing any damage. All they need to do is use biodegradable detergents, separate the household waste and put a solar panel on the roof to solve the problem. They want to have their cake and eat it too. As they say.

It did occur to me right from Day One that a single species out of the many might take the upper hand and subjugate the others. To tell the truth, I thought it would be the lions, or the scorpions, or one of the fighting ants. I wouldn't have bet a nickel on them, those apes playing the smart-asses. Honestly, I thought extinction was their fate: delicate as they are, them and their squidgy, amorphous pups that look like they're made of mozzarella. Instead, they used that Jesuitical guile of theirs to compensate for being vulnerable, and then just hung in there until they had taken down all their enemies including some who were a lot more powerful, leaving nothing but scorched earth behind them. It took them a while, but now they've established their dictatorship and they think it's just how things are. Only, they still need to salve their consciences, and so they're always signing petitions to save whales, Asian tigers, tropical forests, etc., etc.

BIG HANDS ALL OVER THE PLACE

GOD IS NOT the sleepy old fart that many believers imagine—let's get that straight. He likes to keep up with what's going on in the cosmos, he intervenes when he needs to, although intervention doesn't necessarily mean throwing a giant tantrum or staging a Biblical-scale massacre. There are also moments (and these can go on for several million years) during which he just loafs around in his (as it were) slippers. Mostly when nothing much is happening, when the stars are living out their adamantine life cycles, the galaxies evolving as galaxies will, and even on the subatomic level all is going according to plan. When trying hard as I might to come up with something to do, I can think of nothing that can't be done tomorrow. I won't say I sleep, a god never sleeps, but my condition isn't much different from that of a bear in hibernation, or a brumating snake. Let's just say I take things easy.

But then, bang! everything shifts and suddenly I have a thousand pestiferous problems to resolve, millions of things to look after. Rush over here, race over there, put out that, dam up this, patch up the other: I can barely keep on top of it all. And things have gotten distinctly worse since that appalling bungler homo sapiens started making all kinds of trouble: war, epidemics, slaughter, genocide, annihilation. Not only collective disasters but a myriad of individual emergencies. Women starving to death, children mistreated, children put in terrible danger and subjected to agonizing torture. Seven billion individuals, no matter how irresponsible they are, are still seven billion in need of a hand. Sometimes I feel more like a social worker than God. Hardly that high-handed hothead the Bible talks about.

This time, however, there's no holocaust, no fatal siege where the victims have run out of water and their throats burn dry with thirst and fear. There's just a girl whose sexual mores leave something to be desired, a girl who can't stop making herself available. I'm lost here; I can't tear my eyes away from her and I can't understand why. I never dreamed I'd find myself in a mess like this. If it weren't a state as far as possible from divine, in fact quite incompatible with it, I'd say I'm confused.

Around midnight there aren't as many cars coming, and the toads in heat seem to have learned to keep to the right. Don G. has now begun spinning an astronomy lesson for Ms. Einstein's benefit, meanwhile supplying her with ginger-flavored chocolate squares, well-known aphrodisiacs.

Two casual clicks and he switches off their headlamps and begins pointing out the constellations and individual stars, commenting on their colors (indicating temperature), their ages, velocities, varieties of nuclear fission. Speaking in very cogent phrases (it must be said), he discourses at length on the recent discovery of Sagittarius A*. Small as it is, that black hole is a million times heavier than the sun, he informs her, talking the way you would about a sprinter who never loses a race. Raising an arm to point it out to her he nearly grazes her breast—he adores women with girlish breasts—and gives her a blast of the male hormones saturating his breath. She doesn't back away because she's captivated: she, too, a toad frozen in the headlights. All she would have to do to save herself would be to step back—and instead she continues to listen to his singsong spell about the supermassive hole around which the Milky Way's hundreds of thousands of stars revolve.

Bingo, I say to myself as the strapping seducer lunges toward her and kisses her on the mouth. Some things that happen are so predictable that even a drunken tree sloth could see them coming, no need to posit divine intuition. Which doesn't make the matter any less annoying. She doesn't throw herself into it but nor does she push him away, and he, deciding that he now has free rein, pushes her up against the stone wall and lets his hands roam up and down and all over the place. This too is part of the script, of course, but still, she could have given him a shove and run away. Nope, she kisses him passionately in turn, her too-far-apart eyes half-closed, the palm of her hand moving over his chest as if washing a window.

It's pitch dark but I can see the scene as if it were lit up by stage lights, smell the smells: her lips slightly metallic, copper, I'd say, with notes of clove and newborn galaxy.

It's only when the car is almost upon them that they unclutch. So taken are they by their grappling that they don't even hear it; they could have been run over. And the weird thing is, I didn't see it coming either. It's extremely rare that something takes me by surprise, and it feels very peculiar. Their brains are pumped with dopamine and the other sex hormones, the worst drugs out there, and I myself am not feeling perfectly normal either. It's mortifying.

At this point the denouement can only be penetration, over there on the far side of the stone parapet, where there's a grassy patch that seems to have been made for such exertions. The elusive three–three is drawing near. The horny Apollo has seen it now, the grassy little terrace over the lake, and his probabilistic savvy has already weighed the pros and cons. He's calculated the Euclidean distance from the two nearest toad-grabbers and concluded that the sound waves will sink below the threshold of audibility before reaching them. He's checked that the condom in the back pocket of his jeans *for every contingency* is still there. I'm watching, enchanted, about to witness one of those scenes essential to every NC-17 movie.

Instead, without any preamble, she turns on her miner's lamp and, taking plumpish stilt-walker's long strides, heads down the hill to where the wee zoologist is standing. Young Apollo is gobsmacked (and truth be told, I didn't expect this either). He was primed to enjoy the plunge, or at least the solipsistic treat of a *blow job*, (what a term). Now he's worried that this nutcase is off to snitch on him to his girlfriend. He fluffs his dreamy aerodynamic forelock and watches as she

67

becomes a band of light bobbing in the dark. Had he moved too fast? Had he done something wrong? His rock-hard erection is now just a memory.

And so, without being too obvious about it, he begins to move toward them, keeping his ears cocked. His stomach is aching and he badly needs to take a dump.* The geneticist isn't ratting on him, though, just standing by the tiny zoologist picking up toads and putting them down on the valley side of the road with motherly delicacy, giving each one a gentle pat with the backs of her fingers. Her voice is softer and more cheerful, she looks happy there above the lake, its leaden depths streaked white by the moon. He breathes a sigh of relief and glancing at his phone thinks *what luck* (luck, such a detestable concept!) because everything seems to be under control. At that very instant he steps on a toad that's been flattened on the asphalt and slips. As he falls, he hits his elbow violently—I mean very, very violently—and we hear a sound like the neat snapping of a branch.

---

* If there's something that bothers me about men, I mean males, it's their cowardice. They brag and boast, they convince others and themselves they're brave as lions, they go out and blow their entire wages in one night, they show off, pontificate. And then at the first obstacle they revert to being an infant in a diaper: they whine, moan about their fate, beg for some compassionate wing to hide under. From the Get-Go they've all been that way, the only difference is that in the Upper Paleolithic there were no cell phones and social networks to multiply their foolishness.

THE REPOSE OF THE GALAXIES

THIS BUSINESS, so tedious from every point of view, is *extremely concerning*, to employ a lame expression from the small sample I have at my disposal. I'm *thinking* about it—the italics are unavoidable—much too much. That's why I decided on a change of scene today. I decided to wander where my divine feet (atomic reactors?) take me, enjoying the clean air (let's call it that) of intergalactic space, listening from afar to the eternal whirring of elliptical, spiral, and even globular galaxies, the last being the most crowded, that is the most metropolitan. Humans have a somewhat nineteenth-century notion of the cosmos, they imagine a post-Romantic sound-scape, with screaming violins and Wagnerian bellowing; in fact the music of the spheres is more like repeated limpid tinkling interrupted by sharp rustling and the odd explosion, as well as sudden and slightly irritable metallic lacerations.

The few heavenly bodies visible from that modest globe-let called Earth are all very well—Sun, Moon—and they've inspired some earnest, dulcet tunes. Fact is, though, you can see interesting stuff just by looking through a keyhole.

People make do with what they have. However, there's nothing remotely like the heartrending immensity of the universe, gleaming with iridescent lights and palpitating cascades of stars. Not to mention that it's utterly uncontaminated; God willing no intruder's ever going to set foot in it, apart from a few ramshackle earthly space probes with meager range capabilities.

Without meaning to—you may think that's irony, but it's not—I found myself next to two galaxies, one large, one small, that were approaching each other. The deformed shape of the little one, slight but perceptible even to a non-divine eye, like a woman's belly in the fourth or fifth month of pregnancy, made it evident there was an attraction between the two. Later, they would draw closer together and the short, plump galaxy would be sucked in by the large, long one, giving up some of its mass or even being obliterated altogether—always an unsettling event. Now this is *instructive to watch*, I said to myself, *these are cosmic events worth following*. Faced with the—I want to say *choreography*—of the universe, I was recovering the serenity that permeates my heart, call it a heart. No superfluous sentiments, no cloying romanticism, no pointless description needed: what was before me was monumental in its austere abstraction. *I have all the time in the world, I can stay here right to the end*, I thought, positioning myself to obtain the optimal viewing angle and trying to get comfortable, as they say. The way you stretch out your legs to watch one of those long, long art films in which very little happens, indeed nothing at all happens, but which (wo)men of good taste find stylistically perfect.

If anything cheers me up and makes me feel especially divine, it's the interactions between galaxies. It's the elegance of their trajectories, the gorgeous dance numbers executed in perfect detail, their infinite slowness, the sensation of heart-breaking melancholy, but also peace, almost mirth, a tragic mirth that emanates from them, whatever it is, I forget all the rest and feel joyous. Of course, a god is always joyous—what god's a malcontent, a whiner?—but in this case I'm feeling slightly more joyous, because when by definition one is perfect, differences are measured in microscopic gradations.

To tell the truth, though, there was also a sour aftertaste in my mouth that wasn't entirely pleasant (for the purposes of metaphor, let us posit I have a mouth, taste buds). And it was only getting worse. Watching the two galaxies converge, I couldn't help thinking that the beanpole geneticist, too, was heading for a crash, with a body far denser than her own and equipped with much greater gravitational pull. It was a question of mere days and not millions of years, but the highly predictable outcome, as has happened hundreds of billions of times in the cosmos, was that Casanova would either appropriate some of her matter and continue merrily on his way, or he would mercilessly swallow her whole, celebrating with a loud belch.

The very thought astonished me, for never before had the meeting of two galaxies seemed to me a symbol of anything, and it completely spoiled the show. I left the two lovely ladies to their destiny, and headed home. By that I mean the place where I tend to stay, not so much a place as a nexus of the mind, the spirit. What made me *move my butt*, to use a slovenly expression, was the thought that if I stayed there watching to the bitter end, there wouldn't be a trace of the beanpole left. In a few million years, not even a tooth out of the poor thing's mouth would remain. I'd find ranks of crocodiles and other hideous beasties typical of warmer climes, jaws unsheathed. Maybe even iguanas. Thousands of iguanas roaming the industrial plain once inhabited by bipeds, now a swamp, the bipeds extinct. Iguanas with absolutely no sense of humor, iguanas that bite.*

---

* It's pointless to discuss crocodiles, they bite and have always bitten. I made them that way, and I take full responsibility. If I'd done it any other way, we'd have a madly overcrowded animal shelter instead of a food chain, and all of nature would be in chaos. The only proper choice was to have the larger animals eat the small. I couldn't afford to get sentimental about it.

BEAUTY CONTEST

A NEW JOB is opening up in her lab, and Ms. Einstein has made the many photocopies and done the never-ending paperwork to apply for it. Not that she expects to get it, and anyway she's otherwise preoccupied with various mind-bending algorithms. Still, something in her knows she's far better qualified than the others, and she allows herself to think that if she does get it, she won't have the dreadful worry every year that she might be tossed out like old Kleenex. She might count for something, maybe she'll even be able to work openly on her microbe-battery. If she gets it.

But she's not going to get it. I could have told her it was pointless to waste her time filling out all those forms and collecting those notarized statements to confirm she has blood-colored blood and fingernails at the end of her fingers. You didn't need divine insight to figure it out, logic would suffice: the job will go to the new PhD (female) in the lab, who's only been around for a few months but has already earned the protection of the lab director. She hasn't gone to bed with him; rather, her winning move has been to plant a glimmer of hope while *not* having sex with him.* It's also true that she resembles a hot young showgirl seen on TV, a fact that has given her a distinct edge in the grueling job selection process—while Ms. Einstein brings to mind a horse that's grown weary of grazing the same pastures.

But all these goings-on behind the scenes are invisible to her, taken as she is by her clandestine research. She's getting excellent, convincing results now, and many distinguished international scientists have shown interest—that fact alone would disqualify her in the eyes of her roving-eyed boss, if he knew. She's on her way to becoming a sort of Joan of Arc, agog in mystical adoration of Science, ready to wade into battle with her superiors and put herself in danger. She seems to have forgotten all about Casanova and his nighttime kiss. Or rather, every once in a while she does think of him, the way a TV viewer will summon up a few faded memories of a show that didn't leave much of an impression. But you know and I know that little by little she'll soon decide she is attracted to him, then in love, then *truly in love* for the first time. (To use the accepted rhetorical formula, although it seems to have no correlative in human physiology.)

He, meanwhile, thinks about her day and night. This time it's not just a genital thing, it's more than that, he's certain.

---

* It's a solution that works for everyone, for in fact even he doesn't want an affair. Or rather he wouldn't mind the pluses but he wants to avoid the minuses, the danger, first of all, that he'll be found out by his German spouse, who heads a fierce volunteer association protecting battered wives.

The more he thinks about her, the more inebriated he becomes, the more she seems desirable. *By conventional standards she's not beautiful, but in fact, she is,* he thinks. His catastrophic take on climate change has grown less aggressive, more joyful, even slightly ardent. Despite that multiple fracture of the elbow. Unfortunately, the first time they set his bone, the gods of the operating theater were fooling around, and the lad had quite a bit of pain afterward. Human beings are so delicate physically, there's not much you can do about it.

Not that their wandering hands affect me one way or another, although I can't avoid knowing everything they get up to. If they want to marry, have fourteen children, commit joint suicide: it's all the same to me. There are billions of other humans I have to keep an eye on, billions and billions of every type of animal, billions and billions and billions of fascinating stars. Not to mention numerous wars, ruthless terrorist acts, famines and other natural catastrophes whether connected or not to climate change, malaria and cholera hot spots, refugee odysseys, and so forth. It astonishes me that such an intelligent person—so far as intelligence goes, she's smart, no doubt about that—simply does not realize that young Casanova will quickly grow tired of her after he's gotten what he wants, he'll begin paging through his cell phone address book again. And she will be *royally screwed,* to put it crudely. No job and no boyfriend either.

Casanova meanwhile thinks it's time to split from short stuff. The more he thinks about it, the more he finds her ecological fetishes and her dreams of playing the medieval peasant intolerable. But it's a delicate situation; he'll have to move carefully. If he does everything properly, he thinks, she won't cause him problems.

Truth is, she's already *smelled a rat*, because when it comes to this type of thing, the antennae of a human being can out-sense those of a cricket. She saw the games he was playing to stay close to the tall one on the night of the toads, she noticed his testosteronic turmoil when he reappeared, she concluded he'd probably kissed the other, just as he'd kissed *her* a couple of years ago, as he's kissed many others even while they were together, swearing when found out, never again. She ought to be jealous, maybe she is even a little jealous, but much, much less than she had expected. She has to admit she's the first to be surprised.

MY IMMENSE ESTHETIC SENSE

IF YOU THINK God has no esthetic sense, you couldn't be more mistaken. Nope, if there's someone who appreciates beautiful things and will do anything to preserve and promote them, that's me.* You know, if I didn't have this passion for nice things I would have put my energy into function, not form: trees of shapeless gelatin broth, made of a revolting goo like industrial waste. Neon lights that suddenly flick off, instead of sunsets. Bundles of rusty tubes instead of waterfalls; hideous traps baited with smelly hormones to attract insects instead of flowers. Pardon me if this sounds like vanity, but I think I can say I've made a ton of wonders.

---

* Primitive man knew this: they used to make me touching likenesses and nice votive objects. They thought I was a fat lady with abundant thighs and Fellinian breasts and couldn't be persuaded otherwise, although they worshiped me as best they could. When they got a bit closer to the mark, they began to turn out altars carved in the rock, temples, churches, cathedrals, statues in all kinds of materials, frescoes, paintings with sumptuous virgins and bearded saints, rosaries, ostensoria. It's always a pleasure to receive nice presents.

Not one tiresome philosopher (there have been many) has ever maintained that the earth is repulsive and nature dreadful, not one scowling naturalist ever argued that the animal or vegetable kingdom needs to be redone. No twisted poet ever hailed the ocean, or his beloved, as nauseating. All the great men (I might as well say, *all the great ants*, or *all the great lice*) have insisted upon the unbelievable perfection and magnificence of creation, turning out shelf upon shelf of verse and orotund metaphors. I count it this a great success, considering how fussy the humans are.

Frankly, it all stunned me, too. I created and created, unable to stop, and what blew me away, even more than the enormous quantity of species and their crazy variety of shapes and sizes, was the splendor of every single component. Sleek panthers, enchanting palms, hieratic giraffes, proud plovers, gorgeous orchids, the softest, greenest moss, shiny ladybugs, adorable daisies. *Was it really me who created all this magnificence from nothing?* It's all very well being God, but it's one thing to turn out cheesy stuff even if it's perfectly technically sound; it's another to produce pieces that belong in the best art galleries.

Here, it would be nice to be able to calmly view every single element, as people do in a science museum. Keep in mind, though, that it's one thing to come across a lion when you've seen busloads of them on television, another to encounter one at close range when you still know nothing of lions. *Will it bite? Lay an egg? Hibernate?* Of course if I were to think about it I would know the answer, because I know everything, but in the frenzy of creation, I'm no longer sure. When you're creating, there are no cigarette breaks, no union hours. You have to keep turning it out.

Contemporary so-called artists display washing machine parts, driftwood, bodies that have been run through, scrap iron, stones, photographs of genital organs and aged corpses, polystyrene chips, medicine bottles, naked women, even just their own excrement, and the public pretends to be mildly interested. In this age of screens and globalized idiocy, nobody seems to know how to hold a brush. I like paintings where the harmony reminds us that the universe has order, and behind that order, Me. Now if the Architect were someone else (crazy idea) I'd step right up and recognize his/her merits—this isn't vanity. They mesmerize me, the electrons whirling like tireless dervishes around the nuclei of certain minuscule atoms. They send me into raptures, the transparent molecules of water, the perky, stubborn X–rays, the warrens of neat tree trunk cells, the vortices of white hot magma in the heart of the planet. I adore making myself very, very small to zoom around among the quarks as if they were great, majestic weather balloons.

But it's the cosmos that holds the most unforgettable beauties. Lysergic acid, perhaps, might give a human being a pale idea of the glorious sparklings and phosphorescences, the shimmering, kaleidoscopic, ephemeral geometric patterns; the savage smells, some far too strong, others tenuous and vaguely mineral, just slightly more lingering than the faint memories to which they're attached. Who could deny my grandeur before such pageantry? Certainly not the astrophysicists, who insist on peering at the universe from their ridiculous observatories and those spyglasses they think are enormous, who try to get the picture with radar and other feeble instruments.* At times I think I should take them for a spin around the terrifying, fascinating mouth of Sagittarius A*, no need to go much further. They would understand that their sterile sums and calculations are no more illuminating than knowing the number of atoms in a rosebud, they would surrender to beauty, which always comes with its ballast of mystery.

Recently, though, I find myself wrestling with strange questions. What is beauty? I ask, for example. From my point of view, is a beautiful girl (what men think of as a beautiful girl) really beautiful? Obviously not, I tell myself, because when the concept *bella* is applied to a girl, there's a component of trivial carnal desire that offers insight, for anyone who needs it, into the instinctual slums of the human psyche. And I'm not referring to politically incorrect, though frequently employed, expressions like *bella gnocca*, "a nice piece" you might say, to avoid saying something more vulgar. Now if I were to say to someone (although it's absurd to think I might say anything to anyone) that I'd seen a beautiful girl, it would represent an absolute guarantee of integrity; my pretty one wouldn't be just pretty, she'd be morally certified. A virgin, a saint. However, a nice body remains a nice body. How to be sure every element

---

* They're like those who think you can appreciate a beautiful woman from a series of X-rays and sonograms, never sampling the warm fine-grained, elastic skin, the sweet harmony of her curves, the minute but heartrending crevassing of her lips, and so on, all of it made more lovely by her delightful clothes and pleasing trinkets.

gets its proper weight? How to pay tribute to the moral gifts without denigrating the physical side? How to avoid being poisoned by the moral side, which in the blink of an eye turns to moralism, bigotry?

Ms. Einstein, for example, is she beautiful? According to human criteria her hands and feet are too big, her shoulders too broad, face too long, eyes too far apart, mouth too wide, and above all her rear end and thighs are too ample for her to qualify as *a nice piece*. The heavy egghead glasses and the punk Lolita pigtails don't do much for her either. But in my view she has magnificent eyes, splendid hair, great ankles. For me she's infinitely more beautiful than most actresses and models considered *super*.

But can I be sure that this gimpy language hasn't already contaminated me with some human germ, some deadly infection still in its latent phase? No, I can't be sure. Even without wishing to be a prude there's no way I can compare this girl to the alleged mother of my son: virgins don't have so many casual and unplanned sexual relations, they don't steal crucifixes and burn them, don't stay up all night trying to hack the Vatican website. To be perfectly frank—one thing I infallibly am—it's not clear my appreciation of her is one hundred percent divine. And that's making me a little crazy.

THE IGUANA'S PREHISTORIC EYES

JUST AS SHE STEPS over the threshold of the one-bedroom/ animal shelter Vittorio hands her a present: the box of a famous brand of gym shoes (no product placement in my story!) full to the brim with crucifixes. "Awesome!" says Ms. Einstein, running a hand through the contents and flexing her fingers like a fisherman who knows in a flash which are the no-account fish and which the inestimable. "You're fabulous," she adds, continuing to rummage through the Christs, from time to time taking one out to examine it. Euphorically appreciative, she stretches out her long neck and gives him a peck on the cheek.

Of all the things that make me laugh, militant atheists are the funniest. They think the universe gave birth to itself, along with the Earth, the animals living on it, the plants, and of course the humans. Without any help from beyond, any higher purpose, just a *magic wand*—whoosh— and there it all was, working perfectly. They're not alone in this; children, for example, believe their presents come from Santa Claus.

When these same ladies and gentlemen get into their cars they're perfectly aware that the big gizmo that sends them racing down the road didn't build itself, it was designed and put together by someone with skills. They know that the steering wheel and the gearbox, not to mention the engine and the clever anti-skid mechanism, aren't trinkets you can improvise, there's a lot of work behind them. They're not so naive as to think perfection, or something close to it, popped up one night from a cabbage patch. But when they look on a regal sequoia, a slender giraffe grazing, a magnificent heron poised in flight, a breathtaking mountain chain or any other natural wonder (as if *nature* had anything to do with it) no matter how crafted and fine-tuned, they become as silly as penguins and start to mutter about spontaneous generation. Instead of worshiping me, they worship *Evolution*. For that matter even automobiles can be made to seem the product of natural selection. When cars grow bigger, more efficient and more beautiful every day, isn't that thanks to Evolution?

The little zoologist appears delighted that their new friend has dropped by. She seems oblivious to the fact that her partner is a philanderer, just as she's oblivious to the large white cockatoo on her shoulder. The house smells of a truce, like when a couple tires of quarreling. He's proud of his Maoist street cleaner's jacket; his arm is still in a sling. *For some strange reason*, as the traumatologist had said candidly, the fracture was slow to heal. Once the cockatoo has been settled on its perch and the visitor has met the numerous other birds crowded into a large cage next to the refrigerator, they sit down for the meal.

They're eating an appetizer of basil sorbet when Ms. Einstein shrieks and jumps to her feet: she's caught a glimpse of a black and gray snake slithering unctuously across the opposite wall, where the refrigerator stands. It's moving without hurry but decisively, as snakes do. The wee one, instead of screaming, seems happy to see it, like she would a friend who's just showed up after a nap. *He's cute, isn't he?* she says tenderly.

Ms. E. hunkers down in the chair, her feet perched on the cross post. Snakes have always bothered her, she says. Convalescent Casanova shoots her an understanding look. *And that's absolutely normal*, says his expression. *Is it very poisonous?* the tall one wants to know. Somewhat hesitantly, the tiny animal-rights activist acknowledges that yes, it is. Smiling one of her doe-eyed smiles at the cockatoo to reassure him, she explains that it's very rare that snakes bite and even when they do, they usually don't inject their venom. They're very pacific animals, as it happens. Ms. E. asks the seducer if snakes often hang out at their house, and he sighs and says *Yep, twenty-four seven.*

Now if there's an animal I personally have never liked it's the snake.* Sometimes I even think I was mistaken to create them, although once there were moles and mice you needed some type of hungry creature to complete the trophic cycle,

---

* The problem for me isn't that they make me nervous, nor that they represent the bad guys in a certain religion we're all familiar with. I've no intention, with these reflections that nobody's ever going to read, of grinding my own axe here; I was doubtful about these reptiles for many millions of years before those Bible stories came along.

and of course snakes being things that slither on the ground, they can be spotted by large birds from above and snatched up in turn. If I'd given them legs, at the first sign of danger they'd have *legged it out of there* and goodbye carbon cycle closure. If I'd stuck fins on them they'd have jumped in the water, and the birds of prey would have gone home empty-stomached. This is the way it had to be, long flexible salamis with no appendages to facilitate escape and no ears to prick up in response to danger.

The little zoologist asks the big girl if she'd like to touch the viper (he's a *Vipera ammodytes*, aka a horned viper) and without waiting for an answer, she grabs the animal by the neck and picks him up firmly. The beast hangs from her hand like a length of rope and allows himself to be petted like a cat. From time to time, his mouth springs open, but he doesn't seem angry. *You know you're not allowed in the bathroom, 'cause of the mice*, the little one warns the viper as if she were talking to a naughty kid.

The male *hottie* (I fished this tasteless term from Ms. E.'s left cerebral cortex) is telling her that their bathroom is actually an intensive care unit for animals in difficulty. When people in town find a bat with a broken wing or a lame duck, what do they do? They call the city cops, who in turn tell them to consult the Science Museum. Nine times out of ten, the strays that go to the museum end up at their house to be spoon-fed, bandaged and splinted, given their medicines. Badgers hit by cars, baby eagles stunned by high-tension power lines, owls hit with hunters' BBs, foxes vomiting up pesticides, cats fallen from balconies, ducks with bronchitis, insomniac marmots, depressed hedgehogs, et cetera—all have passed through their bathroom. Once the patients are well they're conducted back to their habitat. The iguana, however, is different; he's not going anywhere.

Still holding the viper as if he were a necktie and stroking him, the diminutive zoologist replies that sooner or later the iguana will find a home with someone who loves her. The zoophobic seducer raises two fingers, which seems to mean two years. Each new potential adopter that comes along is ruthlessly rejected—too little iguanaesque fellow feeling. The big lizard continues to scarf down pounds of organic carrots and will probably grow up to be a brontosaurus. Don Giovanni's aiming to sound jovial, but his voice betrays how exasperated he is, or would like to sound.

Would you like to have a look? asks the wee herpetophile. Rather than engage in polemics with her boyfriend, she smiles, her gum-colored gums showing broadly, and addresses Ms. E., who flushes red, the unexpected invitation catching her off-balance. The doe-eyed one now puts the viper on the floor, tapping him on the neck the way you might give your dog a pat. She reassures the cockatoo, who's thrashing his head from side to side like a mad rock star.

The iguana occupies the apartment's lone bedroom, now converted to an iguana pad complete with an infrared lamp to warm the beast. Poised on the highest branch of the leafless tree wedged between floor and ceiling, the thing seems to be asleep; she doesn't move a millimeter, although she stares at them with her prehistoric iguana eyes. *Can I touch her?* the tall one wants to know. The short one says just avoid any brusque movements, you don't know each other yet. She strokes the reptile's back the way she does with her cows, feeling their warmth. The iguana, however, is barely room temperature. The way the beast gazes at her protector, the way the latter in turn plays with the spiky mane behind the reptile's head, it's pretty clear they're involved. It's the cockatoo who's not over the moon; he's plastered himself to his servant's head (that's how he sees her), the feathers on his neck standing straight up.

HUMAN LANGUAGE
OVERWHELMS ME

AT TIMES I don't feel like myself. I was, and continue to be God, I possess all the prerogatives and faculties of a mono-theistic deity—and you can take that to the bank. Although how you take a statement of fact to the bank, as if it were an endorsed check or a jar of pennies, I couldn't say. There are moments now when I fear that things are no longer right with me. I'm annoyed at the snakes (poor things, never did anybody any harm except to get mixed up in the notorious expulsion from Paradise—assuming the story wasn't made up by some bard with a galloping imagination—I myself don't remember anything of the kind). Instead of some more worthy occupation,* I'm here staring, like a fool scientist bewitched by the microbes at the other end of the microscope, at those three in an ugly kitchen on the multiethnic urban fringe of a

---

* There's a range of possibilities, from 1) watching from the presidential box while a star that has run out of gas gets badly crushed by gravity, 2) standing under a shower of X-rays from a white dwarf; to 3) surfing space-time on the back of a gigantic gravitational wave.

tiny planet whirling around a starlet in a little galaxy fancifully named the Milky Way.

In theory it shouldn't matter one blessed iota to me whether this merry-go-round of sexual partners (for that's what this is all about) spins faster or slower, or whether all three of them throw themselves off a cliff or perish in a horrendous car crash. Instead I have a feeling I've waded into something new, something connected with those tawdry mood swings, or rather endocrine swings underlying the bipeds'* melodramatic yearnings, and the messes they make, their stubborn and incurable and *tedious* unhappiness, preparatory to the great collective suicide they're approaching. I find this hard to believe, naturally.

I should stop writing. Stop writing, stop thinking. Things would improve instantly; I'd stop staring at the so-called Milky Way and return to contemplating the cosmos, which after all I'm so fond of. Millions of years would go by without me even noticing, as it used to be. I'd be *in heaven* once again, as they say.

It's a titanic struggle wrestling with a language that wasn't made for a god. Everything I say distorts my *thoughts* (that word!), leads me to utter further nonsense that I don't mean to say and find repellent. My supreme visions and sublime notions emerge as profoundly petty, self-interested and vulgar,

---

* It should be said that in the beginning, they weren't bipeds: most everyone's seen the vignette with the ape on all fours, then crouching, then gradually standing upright until finally he's wearing a necktie. Oh well, I doubt that many theologians would feel comfortable with Adam in the ape phase.

not to say dishonest—pronouncements in which I don't recognize myself at all. I try to dodge every trap, every ruse, to pay more attention, and the result is even more alarming. Some god I am, if human language can overpower me. It's a shattering experience in many ways. As if a god could be shattered!

If I find myself in this regrettable situation it's because I'm a monotheistic deity. If I had some colleagues (or whatever), we would certainly have devised our own irreproachable language, billions and billions of words that zoom around in all directions like sparks rather than follow one another in slavish single file like dumb ants. A three-dimensional language with a syntax that even a hundred thousand years of superhuman effort by the most brilliant linguists wouldn't be able to decrypt. An ethereal parlance, crystalline, utterly free of the sordidness, the ugliness, the pestilence that trails after every human action in a fateful train of electrons. A language that expresses peace and order and harmony. Not one that makes me feel like a deposed king in rags, rooting around in the garbage bins in search of some usable remains.

THE SINKING OF THE TITANIC

BACK AT THE TABLE the three youngsters are eating millet pudding with organic cactus pear garnish that short stuff has prepared, washing it down with the non-organic Turkish wine provided by the neo-punk researcher. *It's just delicious, this timbale with boar ragù*, quips the tomcat. He seems to want to play the comedian to please their guest. *This lamebrain is carnivorous*, sighs the little one, as if she's speaking of something truly gruesome. *You're the only one here who's herbivorous, the rest of us are omnivores*, Vittorio snaps back, looking for complicity in their new friend. She smiles at both, face frozen in a mask of discomfort, as one does when couples pick at each other in public.

The soon to be two-timed zoologist explains that she stopped eating animals when she was still a girl; she couldn't bear to swallow, whether raw or cooked, bits of the corpses of beings that are humans reincarnated, or one day will be. Dead fish have the same effect on her. *I come from a tribe of cannibals, alas; my father was crazy about baby fingers*, her cocky companion butts in. *I know what you mean; I'm not wild about eating meat either, although sometimes I do*, says the lanky one in shorty's direction. The jokester, meanwhile, has turned to stone, his fork frozen in midair.

The wee warrior is radiant. Three-quarters of all the grain cultivated, she points out, is transformed by livestock into manure, obviously inedible, and the animals that produce it also belch out methane, a foul greenhouse gas. Fish are caught and ground into meal, then fed to farmed fish, chickens, and pigs to become millions of tons of more feces, drenched in antibiotics and other highly polluting muck. And the number of the world's carnivores continues to rise, as spirituality declines in poor countries and they convert to globalized cannibalism. And now they're even cloning farm animals, although it's kept hush-hush. The young man, brushing a suffering nineteenth-century artist's lock off his brow, says that cannibalism or no cannibalism, whatever last-ditch solutions people put forward are like trying to resuscitate a dead body. All the climate indicators suggest that the sinking of the Titanic is imminent, even if the dancers in the ballroom are enjoying themselves too much to be aware.

Ms. Einstein gazes at her wineglass as if it were a fortune-teller's crystal ball. Science will come up with answers for all these problems, there's no need to be overly pessimistic, she says. *Scientific research subservient to the interests of the transnational oligarchies will merely accelerate the speed of the driverless race car, soon to smash into the Great Wall of reinforced concrete,* says the tomcat, his brow traced with existential lines. His reaction is unexpected, but he's no shrinking violet, and the hormonal storm underway only boosts his combative spirit.

You do nothing but preach; I've never seen you move your ass one inch, short stuff snaps back.

The Earth will be a toaster in no time, he says, not to be out-done and putting his all into it. *Glaciers will melt like ice cream in the sun, the coastal plains that abut the great metropolises will sink under water, typhoons and other cataclysmic weather condi-tions will be daily occurrences. Nation states will implode in chaos: epidemics, radiation poisoning from obsolete nuclear power stations, bloody energy wars to capture the few oil wells that have not yet dried up.* The bonsai zoologist shakes her head from time to the way one does when one thinks someone is exaggerating, even though the arguments are serious enough.

Ms. Einstein, though, isn't the least bit hesitant. Armored with fundamentalist certainty, she treats him like one more heathen reprobate. Humanity will exploit the sun and the wind, but more important, we will learn to put bacteria and algae to work, she tells him. Bacteria can easily produce the alcohol to fill the gas tanks of our cars, she says, and in the not too distant future they will also produce electricity. The photogenic specialist in climate-change-before-and-after-the-French-Revolution, grimacing like a man with painful hemorrhoids, has decided to go in for the kill. The time is up for all your clever solutions, he says, the great ocean currents are about to reverse direction and half of the earth will soon lie fallow for lack of water while the other half rots at the roots. His girlfriend stares at him, holding her glass in two hands like a child, lips resting on the lip, a tennis player who's been eliminated from the match.

It's hard to say which one of them irritates me most. As far as the future of that little planet named Earth goes, the cocky young wise guy is perfectly right: I myself can scarcely imagine how I would repair such a degraded state of affairs, even supposing that particular bee entered my bonnet.* But he only talks to flatter himself; like many other young fellows he likes to warn us of all the horrendous catastrophes looming, preferably with a glass of wine in hand and some pleasant background music, while privately he thinks the fateful moment is still a long way off, and for some reason won't involve him. Everyone else will die, but he, quite by accident, will survive.

Ms. E.'s scientific optimism annoys me just as much, however. There seem to be no limits to human presumption; from the inception they've been trafficking in flints and other tools (primitive, yes, but still deadly efficient), then moving on to other diabolical contraptions and making them ever more dangerous, so that they could stage their massacres without fear of retribution. And if there's a category of technophiles who with supreme arrogance would like to steal my job, it's the

---

* I'd have to purify the air and the water, cap the hole in the ozone, remove millions of square miles of concrete construction, plant billions of trees, dispose of mountains of garbage and plastic junk, deactivate millions of landmines, bring up dozens of Soviet atomic submarines, resuscitate hundreds of thousands of animal and plant species that have gone extinct, completely restore the entire planet's supply of natural resources: it would be a huge job even for an omnipotent god. But it won't be me. I've done what I had to do and I don't have the slightest intention of starting all over again just because a handful of lowlifes is having a ball destroying everything. It breaks, you pay, as the saying goes.

geneticists. Those necromancers seem to forget that so-called biological life on that insignificant speck of dust of theirs is only possible because of a fleeting set of circumstances that very soon will no longer exist, even before the galaxy takes a hit from Andromeda (what an extravagant name).

But let us not be misled by appearances: what seems to be an argument between the two is more like an amorous display, like the dance elephants do before they mate. Rain or shine, the coitus they crave will soon take place and then the little one, defeated, will retreat. Humans are programmed to copulate, even before they begin to philosophize; the two youngsters certainly don't seem to be an exception to the rule.

The doe-eyed iguana-hugger puts her glass down, and rather than argue with her philandering partner (as would be logical but perhaps counterproductive), tells the other she thinks that in reality every leak that technology plugs opens a larger breach somewhere else. The solution will be to give up all the unnecessary frills, beginning with automobiles (cars merely serve to let you work far from home, work that allows you to buy a more expensive car that allows you to work even farther from home) and television sets and microwave ovens, airplanes and electric blenders, air conditioners and satellite navigators, toilet paper, portable computers, carbonated beverages, high heels. The only thing consumer goods are useful for is to create the phony need for more consumer goods produced by slaves on the other side of the planet, not to mention the continual spikes in overproduction and the dreadful wars. Human beings must take care of the health of their own souls, as well as the souls of the animals and the plants. The rest is just dangerous hogwash.[*]

The super-materialist stares at her as if she's just heard a Martian make a long speech in Martian. She's astonished that someone of her age could unload schlock of that vintage, BS of the kind spouted by that nutcase friend of her mother's. *Without scientific research we could not so much as make a phone call*, she says, tapping a finger on her next-generation cell phone. She sounds not only indignant, but shaken, upset. *Telephones are not only completely useless, they're carcinogenic and should be outlawed*, the little one shoots back.

Tomcat is gloating: each of them is convinced she's right. That way they'll stop putting up that common front of theirs. He figures that he should be able to find an excuse this week to invite the microbe-hugger to have a drink some place with comfortable lounge seats where they can make out like on the night of the toads. Instead of running off this time she'll lure him back to the sexy former fishmonger's where she lives. He can already picture the scene, feel his member getting hard. I can confirm that last point, if you'll forgive me for weighing in where a professional novelist would hesitate to tread.

Our spiritual guides will come to our aid, the doe-eyed one says following a long pause, short of better things to say and showing her gum-colored gums. *Our spiritual guides?* the other

---

[*] For a long time I mistakenly believed that atheists and agnostics were my worst enemies, but recently I've been forced to accept that animism, which I thought was dead and buried, is once again proliferating, if in a new, metropolitan guise.

echoes, face twisted up as if she might have eaten a lemon. *I didn't say religion, I said our guides*, said the first in a low voice, almost an apology for holding such a conviction. *She believes that the souls of the dead and those of the living connect through an Internet-like network, and that some techies somewhere are pulling the strings under the supervision of an extremely powerful secret CEO*, says Vittorio, nodding at his companion with a radiant mocking smile. A pity that just at that instant he is struck by a sudden stab in the gut of excruciating pain, and dropping his dialectical seducer pose he bends over double and begins to whimper like a baby. Men do suffer from the occasional unexpected pain in the gut; it can even be the symptom of a serious illness.

I DON'T KNOW WHAT'S HAPPENING

I DON'T KNOW what's happening to me; Ms. Einstein now seems less odious than she once did. Yes, her devotion to science is a *pain in the backside* (as it were), but watching her play the rutting atheist no longer sets my teeth on edge the way it did; I no longer want to rub her out by sending her bike skidding on an oil stain as she rounds a curve. In some ways, I realize, I'd like to know her better. I mean approach her as a person, not just using my unlimited divine faculties. It would be a less objective kind of knowledge, less complete perhaps, but warmer, more personal.

Instead I listen in on what she's thinking while she rides that big ugly bike of hers, check on what's in her digestive system, how each of her hairs is coming along, whether the pores of her skin are dilating and contracting properly. I flip through her past the way you page through the photo album of a family member you are particularly fond of, going back a couple of generations—even a dozen while I'm at it. I study the workings of her genes (genes being not nearly as boring and conservative as geneticists think) and the cordial ententes that link them to the amino acid sequences of every protein in every cell. Not that I neglect my normal divine duties: I surveil, I resolve, I save, I punish, I overlook, I admonish, I judge, I unleash, I even avenge (that happens sometimes, my son, or presumed offspring, notwithstanding). However, it's her above all whom I scan.

I myself am astonished at what's happening to me. I look at myself in the mirror (metaphorical mirror, *ça va sans dire*) and I see that I'm the same, I'm what I've always been. I'm still absolutely perfect, absolutely no doubt about that: I remain infallible, omniscient, omnipotent, omniwhatever. And yet, and yet . . . I'm unable to transcend this damn Daphne (that's her name), sympathetic or not; I follow the evolving situation attentively (I almost said *greedily*), not missing a single minute of it.

But the randy paleoclimatologist, despite those health problems of his,* is playing a tight defense. His latest thing is to send her text messages, and, one excuse after another, he's constantly tapping away. His comments, meant to be witty and captivating, are in fact merely stupid, but she reads them all right through, sometimes even laughing to herself. You don't have to be a god to see how that devious electronic tomfoolery

---

* The stomachache that suddenly intervened during the meal with the iguana turned out to be rather serious; he vomited all night, thrashing around in pain. In the morning he was even worse and they hospitalized him for a couple of days to do tests. Alas, the health of a human being is always hanging by a thread, the tiniest factor can put everything out of whack.

might well be the final offensive in his campaign to take his coveted target. The cleft between her legs, that is.

His companion, meanwhile, seems to be forcing herself to do exactly the opposite of what *common sense* would dictate. Having sussed out the danger, anyone else in her situation would go out of her way to keep her rival as distant as possible, put her partner under lock and key and threaten him with all manner of retribution. Instead, she's constantly calling the tall biker to suggest they do this or that. She's wild about those crazy rides on the priapic twin-cylinder. I won't say I'd be pleased if she took an electric knife and removed her boyfriend's filthy big tongue—excessive violence has never appealed to me, whatever's been said about that—but still, she could at least give him an ultimatum or threaten to throw him out of the house. Instead, she's as obliging as a little lamb.

HARBINGER RITUALS OF SEX

ON HER BIRTHDAY Ms. Einstein gets to her lab at 2 a.m. For several hours she focuses all her concentration on a new prototype of the bacteria-powered battery, a model that encompasses everything learned so far. Sucking on slivers of candied ginger, she adds nutrients and the agreed-upon inocula, sets the temperature and the pressure, and programs the survey of electrical conductivity and other factors at established intervals. She likes the rapt silence of nighttime, likes to feel the energy of dawn's first glimmers on her, when the birds begin to stir on the blighted grounds around the Institute. She doesn't yet know what will come out of this, but the back of her neck and the lining of her lungs tell her it will be very interesting. Those are points whose sensations she trusts.

When she's finished taking samples of genetic material she returns all the equipment to its place and hides the battery, which unfortunately is quite a bit more voluminous than the earlier one. In the meantime the laboratory is filling up, and the young pretender with the phosphorescent pimples sits down in front of the atomic absorption spectrometer, aiming his pleading looks her way, something she can't bear. At a certain point the lab director also shows up but she doesn't notice him, so taken is she with the article she's writing, not to mention the South African rap music blasting through her earbuds. The boss coughs politely, shifting a foot to one side as if to crush a harmful insect. That Catholic vibrato is familiar to her and she raises her eyes from his elegant shoes to his well-rested face, his phony indifference masking memories of their intimacy, so out of place. He smiles, showing all his teeth.

While she's removing the earbuds he's describing a job he wants her to do, his short stout hands (mole's paws, she thinks) making wide circles in the air to accompany his words, which repeatedly contradict what he's just said, even as his traffic-cop gestures struggle to make them come together in a single ordered flow. She doesn't understand a thing, it being materially impossible to understand. She'd be amazed if she did. Patting his firm cheek (smooth as a baby's butt, she thinks), he concludes by saying that in fact it isn't urgent. He then smiles intently at her with his baby eyes, as if he's very pleased with her reply (she hasn't said a thing). The 15,000-rpm centrifuge where their two-zero took place is just a few yards away, but their eyes don't stray toward the spot where that kinetic frenzy occurred.

The reason he's so affable is that the hiring committee for the job she'd applied for had met the previous day. And he, president of the committee, wielding his usual flutter of jokey remarks had got everyone to agree they hire the one who looks like the TV showgirl. So it's she, so clever at dispensing smiles and glimpses into her cleavage, who'll be hired, while the beanpole will be out on the street. There's not enough extra in next year's budget to keep her on as an adjunct. The boss doesn't regret what he's done, no. There will be many fewer articles published, but his life will also be considerably less stressful. His rather severe German wife is now also working for the courts, where so many divorce cases come up. As a good Catholic, though, he feels ever so slightly uneasy, which is why he's come by to interrupt her.*

At lunchtime Daphne heads off on the bike to inseminate a dozen Friesians. She's slightly late and has to pass up the usual couple of *bignè alla crema* from the pasticceria right on the main road, the ones she particularly likes. The cowshed, in a town not very distant from the city, is quite large and bordered on three sides by abandoned industrial shells. They already know her here and they trust her, so she's left alone. As she introduces an arm into the anus of the first Friesian she's thinking that the wee zoologist isn't entirely wrong: it would be better not to eat animals. But these are dairy cows, not beef cattle.† Still, her friend would be horrified if she saw

---

* Despite their reputation as irreprehensible, Italian Catholics are capable of the most nefarious behavior, even toward friends and closest relatives. Afterward, though, they suffer strange abdominal upsets not unlike digestive problems, and try to make up for it with hypocritical smiles and witty remarks while they prepare to clear their criminal records by visiting the confessional booth.

† With that incoherence so typical of human thought (an intrinsic *cerebral opportunism*?) she's not counting the fact that dairy cows, when their milk days are up, are also sliced and ground. And never mind about the male veal calves.

the assembly line conditions here. For the first time she feels uncomfortable.

On the way home she stops at her usual garage. Since the last time the bike was repaired it's been running fine, but all the same she puts it up on the kickstand in the square and goes inside. The owner tells her that the mechanic who worked on it has gone to race an Enduro. So she sits down to wait on her doubly erect twin-cylinder and looks at the other bikes parked around hers, imagining how she would improve them. She's never studied mechanical engineering but she knows enough to mentally scan a bike body or engine quickly, identifying structural defects and little flaws. When the mechanic with the boxer's flat nose shows up she smiles at him and says she's reconsidered, and would like to do that checkup he was proposing. They discuss the terms for a few minutes, then she's off. She stops in a church she often visits—and here I must ask that we cast a veil over what she's up to—and then to the supermarket.

Back home in the old fishmonger's, she begins cleaning house. It's that type of ruthless cleaning that precedes some very important occasion, some special party. She polishes the two big windows facing the inside court where the old entrance to the fishmonger's was, she shines up the inclined surface where the fish were laid out, now her kitchen counter, removes the three-quarter mattress from the old trout basin, vacuums, disposes of the dust balls from the coils of computer cords, washes the sky-blue tiled floor. You can see it's not a burden, that she's actually happy to clean up. She folds the balled-up clothes lying around, dusts the knickknacks atop the "furniture," changes the cat box, for which the cat, though blind, seems to be grateful. Now she's working on the atmosphere: incense, candles, plates of biscotti and candied ginger like votive offerings.

You'd think she was arranging a sacred ceremony, while it's nothing but a banal copulation. Sex for sex's sake, without even the appearance of moral pretext (never mind the institution of the family and the ceremony that seals it). When I think of this I feel a hard-to-define discomfort, a pang I don't think I've ever felt before, almost misery. This is depraved materialism at its worst, unfolding in a context where the individual and his/her corporal nature are fetishistically sacralized under the specious sombrero of *sexual freedom*. But am I not partly responsible, when I allow them to copulate in that wild way the randy one favors? Doesn't that mean I've given her a sort of license?

It would be child's play for me to blow young Randy's plans to smithereens. I mean, what does it take to knock down a bicycle ridden by a guy with one arm in a sling and mysterious stomach pains, just as an old van whose brakes are shot comes along—or better, might as well do things properly—a tractor trailer? The cyclists are asking for it, in a way, trying to glide through the anarchy of Italian traffic. It often happens without me raising a finger. A hard blow to the temple, I'm thinking; no blood or other distressing fluids. Just a cranium smashed in at the parietal lobe. *Fate can be so cruel*, people would whisper. *At least he didn't suffer, poor guy*. All those agnostic remarks that by now no longer even touch me.

I'm ready to intervene. I already have the bike in my cross-hairs, and needless to say, it's red. I'm merely waiting while the rider,* who's now bent over the seat, gets on and begins to pedal. I'm rubbing my hands with glee (forgive me if I turn up the hype, a story shouldn't be boring) the way every killer does. I sense the slight tension in me that marks the approach of the *fatal hour*. I'm already feeling slightly better because this nightmare (so it seems to me at times) will soon be over. I'll be back to my old self; I'll cease to think about these matters once and for all. I'll take up my old duties.

But then, as Daphne meticulously bathes her long asymmetrical body, I reflect that the situation that's been created (by whom? I need a break here) is utterly ridiculous. Whatever it may say in the Bible, where there's entirely too much emphasis on those rare occasions when I lost my head, I believe in being fair and impartial. And it's obvious that I would completely disqualify (not to say something much saltier) myself if I were to behave like some grandee pursuing only his own interests. In time the word would spread, and with it, complaints and protests. In the long run no one would believe in me, and atheism would triumph.

---

* Perhaps someone will think I'm the mastermind (so to speak) behind his fractured elbow on the night of the toads. That is utterly untrue. Here is what actually happened. When I saw that he was about to step on a very slippery spot (a toad flattened by a car tire) I slightly corrected the spin of his fall to prevent him from putting his hand down in the same slimy mess. Now it's true that he smashed his elbow instead of dirtying his hand, but my intentions were nothing but the best, as befits a merciful god.

I therefore surrender to my own infinite wisdom, and put down the (metaphorical) high-power precision rifle. The red bicycle will not be run over, at least not on account of any *special* intervention of mine. If a tractor trailer involved in an *ordinary* accident were to crush it, that would be another kettle of fish. Meanwhile the old fishmonger's will once again be transformed into a temple of sex and host the nth profane sexual congress. I can do nothing about it.* Take it up with the Last Judgment.

* I want to be sure this point is crystal clear: although I ultimately pull the strings of all that takes place in the cosmos and on tiny planet Earth, there are many details that I leave to so-called *chance* to arrange as it sees fit and proper. Amen.

A STROLL AROUND THE COSMOS

FOR A *CHANGE OF SCENE* I went out once again (meta-phor!) for a stroll among the galaxies. I didn't want to know another thing about the big girl in heat and what she was up to or not. I am God, not a peeping Tom, or some kami-kaze friar raring to detox the little planet from its poisonous techno-consumer drug habit, its allergy to transcendence in any shape or form, and its obsession with sexual gratifica-tion. She can copulate with whomever she wants, that godless creature with her far-apart bird eyes. Let her be tortured in bondage gear or sodomized by a rhinoceros, it's all the same to me. *I'm going to calm down now*, I thought, but in fact I was getting even more upset.

However, once I'd put a couple billion light years between me and the Earth (and its inescapable familiarity with evil) I began to feel better. The way a person befuddled by stress abandons the chaos of a metropolis and slips into a peaceable forest (I'm trying to draw a parallel here that can speak to everyone) I was able to rest my eyes and ears and empty my brain of every last thought. It did me good, as getting down from a train benefits the passenger—and wormholes through space-time are not so different from a railroad train—it did me good to idle through that awesome gallery of gargantuan abstract paintings, or perhaps I should say surrealist. Full of innumerable chromatic nuances, but as always violet and emerald green, watery ocher tints shading into pearl gray: my favorite colors as far back as the Creation. Among colors I include infrareds, which bring a pleasant warmth to the skin (those that have skin), and X rays, so energizing, like intravenous caffeine, a soft drug. And then there are radio waves and their odd, enigmatic cacophony, like contemporary electronic music played at the bottom of a cave heard by an ear plastered to an aperture at the mouth. When I refer to colors, it's merely a figure of speech.

Dillydallying without any precise destination, I came upon a blue star. Blue, like Daphne's eyes, I found myself thinking. It was magnificent, a precious stone set in the cosmos. Splendid in a way that was also heart-wrenching, that made one apprehensive, perhaps because blue stars are such ephemeral things: four or five million years and they're gone. Contemplating them, it's impossible not to think of this tragic fact. As I'm sure you're aware, a god's not compatible with a cell phone, or I would have snapped a photo.

I then passed near one of those elderly stars on which humans have slapped a name that might better suit a discotheque out in the sticks. Supernova. The light coming off that colossal explosion was so blinding I almost regretted not having my sunglasses (truth is, I never wear them, so

New Age). Even an amateur stargazer knows that these old boilers host deadly fission explosions compared to which the nuclear weapons that humans are so afraid of are harmless firecrackers.

It was quite hot, although I don't suffer from the heat, and I don't sweat either. The stellar storm was so devastating it would have ripped out my hair, if I had hair. Immateriality does have some advantages. The chemical scents—roasted manganese, and especially sulfuric acid, with underlying notes of methylcyanoacetylene—were nice, admittedly, but truly very *strong*.

It does make you think: that immense ball of light brighter than hundreds of millions of their Suns, apparently the quintessence of life, was actually in its death throes. A blazing and utterly splendid demise, but still a last hurrah. Why things appeared this way to me, why it made me so uneasy to think of death, I couldn't say. Maybe all this expressing myself in the human mode had contaminated me? It distressed me (and I'm the first to be amazed here) to think that Daphne would very soon be deceased.

Now don't let yourself succumb to melancholy thoughts, I told myself: the dust spat out by that fearsome Roman candle will give birth to other stars, maybe even more beautiful, and those will bring forth others. Oh, and check out the cheerful *happening* involving that group of black dwarfs to my right—in front of the ravenous mouth of a black hole—pulsing, spinning, shrinking, extending their arms and shaking their hips like great dancers. One of them had psychedelic concentric halos, like a phosphorescent onion wearing fifty brightly colored windbreakers one on top of the other; another with huge owl eyes, great reflecting mandalas; a third like an hourglass full of neon tubes of all colors. It was like, correcting for proportion, being at the Carnival in Rio, or one of the Gay Prides.

Just look at all the gorgeous galaxies I've created! I thundered, thrilled with what I saw and very proud to be God. *I am God*, I said, enjoying that feeling you get contemplating something you've made with your own hands, the satisfaction of a job well done, of time well spent. Of course the euphoria of a god has nothing in common with human pride; it's steeped in perfection, it's perfection itself. However, the immediate sensation was in some ways similar, and a whirl of great ideas spun through my head, a myriad of plans for the future.*

Wandering about, nowhere in particular, I came upon two spiral galaxies of about the same size, engaged in that step back they take after they've completed the courtesies of the first approach, a step that portends actual fusion. As often happens at this stage of the collision, they already had a tender brood of just-born stars between them, the little ones palpitating and bickering like chicks bursting with infant energy. Even the high-pitched crackling sounds they made from their nest, protected from the great stellar winds provoked by the

---

* Before I began this diary, I'd never been aware of having highs and lows, or maybe I was simply always in the same gelid mood. Talking and thinking, one ends up getting confused.

embrace of the parents, sounded like the cries of famished infants. Later, one at a time, each would set out on its own solitary way, at times a fatal one even in the prime of life, but for now they were reveling in careless youth.

That family portrait, so joyous and tender, touched me deeply. For the very first time I felt an indescribable turbulence inside, something like a father's yearning, or perhaps a great-grandfather's. But when I examined the feeling, there was in my languor (I can't think of a more suitable word I could pick from the lexicon's shallow little cauldron) a sort of nostalgia for something I'd have liked to have and didn't have. I don't know, someone to chat with once in a while, a friend to talk to in despondent moments. If not actually a family, children. They weren't very divine emotions, banal as they were. But they were such sweet sensations that I couldn't shrug them off.

THE AMOROUS LITURGY

APOLLO'S KNOCKING at the door of the old fishmonger's as expected, and improvident Daphne is now about to open it. She's wearing a tunic down to her feet that shows off her nipples through the fabric, the side seam split nearly to the hip. This intangible veil is meant to disappear from circulation quickly, but even if it doesn't it won't get in anyone's way. Vittorio, drenched with sweat, had been a little bit low, but seeing how she's got herself up, he now feels better immediately. He can surmise—and I know for certain—that the bushy mound of her pubis is right beneath the gown. He tells her he was in the neighborhood by chance (at that time of day?) and thought he'd drop by and say hello. He doesn't mention that the afternoon began with a flat tire, and he then had to walk the bike all the way over in the muggy, burning afternoon heat while he ruminated on the various woes afflicting him lately. Those *inexplicable* stomachaches that he just can't get rid of, and sometimes the pain darts up his back and all the way down to his heels. It's still preferable to being mutilated by a tractor trailer, but he doesn't know about that or even suspect

113

it. Gathering his courage, he advances, in high feline pelvic slouch, toward the amorphous sack filled with polystyrene chips that Daphne calls her sofa.

The beanpole, planted on legs not very powerful yet plump-ish, regards him the way you do a handsome actor, with a certain deference that would like to be chaste but is helpless to defend against his charms. He senses her admiring gaze on his high Risorgimental brow and, eyes trained on the floor, seems to want to apologize and tell her there's nothing he can do about it, this is the lot he's been assigned. His white shirt is now open to the sternum, framing his wide, flat chest like a stage curtain. On his feet, beach flip-flops point to the precariousness of the light clothing he's wearing, insubstantial as leaves that might flutter away at the first hint of autumn breezes.

The lights are low in the former fishmonger's, and a large, stubborn candle sends out sensuous smells and tremulous glimmers, never mind its ecclesiastical provenance. There's a comfortable tatami mat on the floor that if need be will deftly support two twined bodies, and near it—by chance?—a packet of tissues. Every little detail has its place: the blind cat cuts across the room with the lightest of footsteps. When the gong sounds, she'll disappear, she promises.

The shameless girl lights a stick of incense that smells of tawdry sandalwood and oriental spices. If there's one thing I can't bear, it's the fumes of burning *Boswellia sacra* resin. As she passes by, she taps the lamp clipped to the edge of the fish basin to dim the room's lighting even further. Now, not letting herself be seen, she rolls her far-apart camel's eyes about. In that neoclassical tunic she might be a high priestess checking that all is ready before she begins the ceremony. The victims chosen for the pyre are standing by the altar, the temple smells of balsam, spirals of smoke rise from the torches toward the sky, where the pagan gods are meant to reside.

The sly fox takes out the book he brought on the connections between climatic catastrophe and social revolution. (But didn't he just stop in by chance?) He thinks he might grab her and pull her close with his good arm, seeing that she's kneeling by his side, pleased that he's brought her a present, blushing a little, pressing her long thigh against his knee. But her sparkling smile seems to say she'd prefer to follow the normal path prescribed in the amorous liturgy, no shortcuts, so he hands her his offering, an oblation to placate Aphrodite. She nods and presses the bible of revolutions sparked by climate change against her very small breasts, as if the book were a gift from the Magi. *Thank you*, she murmurs, her throat already swollen with desire. He narrows his eyes lazily, the way a cat does when scratched on the side of the neck.

At this point he's just about to lay his unsplinted arm on her shoulder; a silent countdown is underway. Minus three, minus two, minus one—but then, one millionth of a second before zero, she leaps to her feet, arching forward as elegantly as a dolphin leaving the water. Would he like a glass of rum? *Classic*, I think: she'll give him a strong drink—not strictly necessary—and that will be the dynamite to bring down the last bastion of a city that in fact has already surrendered.

Apollo accepts gladly, and, fluffing up his Giuseppe-Verdian locks with his good hand, rattles the two ice cubes in his rum to make the glass ring solemnly.

His swollen lower lip brushing the edge of the glass, he asks casually if she has anything to do that evening. She's wearing an equally neutral face, to suggest that the idea of *spending the evening together* (to employ that figure of speech) is something that just came to her. But now she clears her throat and says very firmly that she's waiting for her aunt and they have to discuss something that's a bit of a nuisance. And *unfortunately she'll be here any minute*, she says, looking at the time on her phone. He's stunned, and wonders if he heard her right. To tell the truth, I'm not sure I understood her either.

The purple-pigtailed priestess is now standing in silence, the way you do when you're waiting for someone to make up his/her mind to leave. She compresses those wide horizontal lips of hers, and begins to paw the floor like a hungry mare. So he gulps his rum and starts for the door, head down, a boxer with an out-of-commission arm who has taken a hail of blows. That confident smile of his is now just a vague memory. He really can't make out where he went wrong; everything was flowing as smooth as oil from a jug and then suddenly he'd been expelled from the game. She squeezes his good arm affably, the way you send off the Jehovah's Witnesses, and shuts the door smartly behind him.

My legs seem about to buckle under me, although a god doesn't have legs and if he did, they would be very sturdy. What's happening to me? I don't know, only that nothing like this has ever happened before, which is why I'm so confused. It's as if I've had a brief *spell*, one in which you lose consciousness for a few seconds.

At the same time I'm relieved, and can once again breathe normally (figure of speech). So relieved I'm close to tears (same). Daphne had not been preparing some demonic orgy, as I'd feared; she hadn't dressed to facilitate coitus, the mat on the floor meant nothing. Or maybe it did, but then she hesitated, and her best side came forward and she resisted (in extremis, it is true) the terrible temptation. Sure, she's a bit of a libertine, even for these pornographic times, but apart from a few episodes of undeniable intemperance, she's not a loose woman, she never has been. One day, maybe not too long from now, she'll even rethink her views about Me.

I ask myself, how did I get the picture *so ass-backwards* (ridiculous expression); what prevented me from seeing how things were going to turn out? What's become of my proverbial foresight? Of course, anything can happen, but a god cannot allow himself to be so badly led astray by appearances. For a god, present and future are one and the same, they're just two pages in the book before him. With hindsight it's obvious my mind was clouded; sometimes one has to be frank about these things. But hey, let's not focus on the negative. What matters is that it all ended well.

BEDEVILED BY STRANGE THOUGHTS

LATELY I'M BEDEVILED by strange thoughts. I think I'd like to be a man. A real human being, not a god incarnated in a man; no matter how skillfully executed, a deity embodied in a human always retains something of the divine. I'd like to be a man who has just one idea at a time and not the faintest notion of why he's on this earth, or what the point of his existence is. A canonical biped perennially unhappy about one thing, anxious about another, always hungry or thirsty or sleepy or hurting somewhere, who can flip in an instant from euphoria to darkest misery.

In these strange moments I imagine I'd like to know for certain that I would die, and that so would everyone else around me. Without knowing when and how, without being able to do anything about it. To be a man is certainly a miserable condition, really quite mediocre, and from a certain point of view, brutalizing, dehumanizing, but also very romantic, it seems to me. I don't mean to be a man for eternity—that wouldn't even be possible except by constantly changing bodies—but long enough to satisfy the urge. To try out among other things those elusive sexual stimuli that loom so large in their existence. To get drunk on wine, sampling all the best wines in existence at once, and all the beers, and a representative sample of spirits. To experience great happiness, and immediately after, tremendous sadness, and so forth.

Some quiet, frigid evenings, when I'm passing through a dark nebula's silicate dust-cloud, I *close my eyes* and imagine I really am a man. No longer a god but a *homo sapiens* of the male gender who *through a series of coincidences* comes into contact with the thin-on-top and heavy-at-the-bottom girl. Obviously I won't tell her who I really am; she wouldn't believe me, she's an atheist. I'll also stay away from any subject that has anything to do with theology, and I'll pretend to forget, or almost, the most important things, as the most erudite humans do, and I'll have loads of prejudices and idiosyncrasies. I'll pretend to speak just a handful of languages, badly, and as far as genetics goes I'll listen to her as if I haven't a clue what she's talking about, not a clue, as her acquaintances do. On the other hand I mustn't exaggerate in the opposite direction or I'll be taken for an imbecile. I must also shine, fascinate her. A difficult balance for someone accustomed to excelling.

On reflection, perhaps the gravest danger is that she'll think I'm a simpleton. That would really be something if she saw me as unattractive and I ended up in the same class as her colleague with the sunset-colored pimples. Once I wrangle my way in, her first impression will be all-important and all but impossible to alter—even for omnipotent me.

At this point, just to reassure myself, I flood a stretch of superhighway and bring down a commercial airplane. *The cause of the crash could not be determined.* However, the fears and uncertainties soon creep back.

Maybe *confused* is an exaggeration, but I find my reasoning disturbed, my thoughts quaking, wound up in corkscrews like those of a staggering drunk. I hope I'm mistaken, but I fear these are the egoistical charms known as *feelings* in which the bipeds have been indulging ever since I created them. I knew right away that something was amiss. I try to chase the things off but they just cling there, corroding my divine aplomb like sly woodworms. I had no idea that such a thing could happen.

DEMON SEX

SOMEONE'S KNOCKING on the door of the old fishmonger's shop. Again. Has the handsome climatologist returned? Sprained his ankle walking his bike in that dreadful heat? Typical questions a scribbler likes to pose. But apart from a bad headache (too much excitement) on top of the stomach-ache and the broken elbow, everything's fine with Apollo. Nor can that be an aunt rapping, no matter how testosteronic her biceps; this is the energetic, imperious hammering of an impatient (maybe even violent) hominid. Daphne, however, goes to open the door without concern, and does not seem at all surprised to find the mechanic who fixed her bike. The burly one with the prizefighter's nose.

Yes, it's him, although he's not wearing the usual overalls with the Japanese logo on the back. He's dressed in very tight pale-blue jeans and a tight red T-shirt that clings to knots of bulging muscles that look carved in wood (a bodybuilder, is my guess). On his feet, a pair of oversized gym shoes, like a kid might wear. She barely has time to take in these details, though, because he immediately grabs her head, as if taking possession of the thing he came for (it was clear he hadn't come for the conversation). She lets him take her mouth without hesitation, as if fearful of crossing him. She also allows his hard, rough hands to slip inside her tunic, indeed she expedites their imperious advance by moving her upper body in concentric circles, moves that resemble the undulations of a cunning snake. When the big hands find her nipples she grips his biceps with all her strength, as though seeking his protection in a situation of grave danger.

Minutes later they're on the mat and her tunic is an open book, and not a holy one. Spread over her long body, the mechanic pumps his mighty arms as his pelvis delivers potent thrusts, the way he might pound a large post into the ground. He looks like he's in a hurry to complete a strenuous task. She, meanwhile, cheek glued to the sky-blue floor tiles, stares out the bayonet window open to the alley of the Nigerian prostitutes, her vision clouded as if she's about to faint. She seems almost unconscious, or drugged. Alone in a world of wind and bright sunlight.

Now the bike shop satyr slams harder, he seems to want to break right through the floor and descend into the cellar. (Inferno, I think. Inferno was one of the many hobbyhorses of that supposed son of mine, but I must give him credit, the scenography was undeniably powerful.) Finally the satyr emits a long braying sound, an asphyxiated donkey desperate to catch its breath. He hovers over her for a few seconds, tremors running through him like an epileptic fit, then deflates on top of her. Maybe those rock-hard muscles broke something inside him? It's another one–zero, but this is merely act one. The mighty tool has only contracted by a few millimeters; he just needs a short break. It won't be a night of verbal disquisitions or philosophical conjecture; in fact, they're looking in opposite directions. She, toward the post-Fordist courtyard behind the wall of glass bricks; he, toward the plate of biscotti on the rim of the fish tank.

DIABOLICAL COLLATERAL DAMAGE

AS FAR AS I CAN REMEMBER (false modesty—my memory is murderously infallible) I've never made an error before. I mean, never. Sure, there were times when I massacred innocents, but I have never misread the facts so badly, have never outright mistaken one thing for another. This time I really *dropped the ball*. All the evidence was before my eyes, but my divine gifts were knocked out by a tempest of *feelings* (I don't know what else to call them), the way those electronic gadgets scramble an enemy's radar. The licentious lassie had arranged her tribal sex session not with the handsome hunk who's struggling like a fly on flypaper, but with the muscular mechanic (and the outcome was a very disappointing four–zero to boot).

This situation must come to an end. I've said it and I repeat it: while the concepts of time and space-time don't apply to me, when something keeps happening, it *keeps happening*, and one can't pretend otherwise, something must be done. I can't let my entire existence, or whatever you want to call it, be reduced to nonsense by one specimen of the human race, and not even one of their best. She's no ascetic consumed by a mystical flame, no paragon of devotion who lowers her eyes and endures the worst torture of the flesh; if she were, that would make up for the various sins and defects we've observed. No, she's a militant atheist who spends her nights trying to sabotage the Vatican website (recently she found a chink in the armor, and I fear the worst). She's an incorrigible misbeliever who's in favor of gay marriage and abortion on demand—something she's practiced herself not once but twice—and all she cares about is her own sexual satisfaction. And never mind that her precious satisfaction is by no means guaranteed, as evidenced by the paltry tally earned in her pornographic brawling. She's obsessed with sex. A witch, in short, who in another time and place would have been burned at the stake. Nothing like this happens even in the filthiest trashy novels.

It's the collateral damage that's the worst, however: worse even than the direct harm. The consequences for my state of mind. I *can't sleep a wink*, my thoughts grow ever more labyrinthine; my faultlessness less crystalline and exemplary. I'm a pioneering example of faulty faultlessness, a terrible headache for dialectical philosophers. It's not so much the age difference—I have no age—nor that of rank, for my rank can't be compared with any other, but a god is a god, and a human a human. I risk making myself ridiculous for all eternity, should anyone find out. I'll go down as the god who lost his head for an atheist who sticks her arm up cow's asses and incinerates crucifixes. *Stop!* I think, *I'm raving mad! My thinking is deranged. This can only bring disaster!*

For billions of years (if not even more; truth is, I never kept count) everything went as smoothly as oil from a jug. I kept an eye on things, I attended, I superintended, I rewarded, I contained, I punished (I don't mind admitting it), I threw fits (yes, it happens). All this was business as usual for a unique god who, because he has no employees or colleagues, must hoist the whole weight of the cosmos on his shoulders but succeeds brilliantly because he's omnipotent. But now I hesitate, I dither, I procrastinate.

I wonder if I might be slightly depressed. These days most men are demoralized; they've boxed themselves into a corner, and in the course of sitting here watching them, maybe I've caught some similar ailment. The difference is, of course, that I can hardly go to some therapist and say, Hello I'm God and I'm not feeling so great. Even Freud himself couldn't help me. I mean, a lame elephant could scarcely expect a presumptuous Austro-Hungarian gnat to keep him on his feet. Not to mention that ninety-nine percent of psychoanalysts are atheists, which implies a surreal scenario: an atheist having an amiable conversation with God. Nor could I swallow antidepressant pills (How many? Certainly the label would not include the optimal dosage for the undersigned). A god must always resolve matters himself, whatever happens, whatever mess he gets into.

It's this "diary"—N.B. not one *day* has ever gone by for me out here—that's bringing me to ruin. You write, and the more you write the dizzier you become, and you end up with a headful of foolishness. Your reason begins to unravel, you fall in love. It's been happening since the beginning of time to millions of boys and girls in their sad little rooms but also to ranks of adults, even eminent seniors, oblivious to the ridicule they invite. All of them dishing out sticky, sentimental phrases, choking back sobs and wetting their keyboards—once sheets of paper, before that papyri—with hot tears stirred up by the same silly whimpers the keys of their computers make (previously fountain pens and before that quills and styluses). And now it's happened to me. *God or no god.*

WHERE THE SNAKES LIVE

THE SNAKES live in the scree heap at the bottom of a gray rock face still shielded from the sword-strokes of the rising sun. *A real den of snakes*, thinks Daphne, a long shiver running up her spine. Behind her, the wee zoologist hops gaily from one stone to the next. They're so quiet that two roe deer at the edge of the woods graze unafraid. Not even the shadow of a snake is visible yet, but the tiny explorer isn't concerned. *Plenty of snakes*, she whispers, smiling to one side as you might when speaking of a particularly dear friend. And in fact, less than two minutes later she is holding one in her fist. The beanpole has no idea where she found it, because she was looking the other way. The sprite is holding it like a belt, not taking special precautions, but delicately, so as not to damage the horn in the middle of its forehead.

Daphne had spent the whole day previously, Sunday, at the lab, as well as all night. Twenty-three hours straight with only two breaks for three chocolate bignè and a bag of peperoncino-flavored potato chips that she'd found on the shelf of the pimpled chemist who wants to marry her and have ten kids. Oh, and three packets of candied ginger. When she got to the meeting place in front of the Greek herbalist's and caught sight of the little one's doe eyes and gum-colored gums, all her fatigue slipped away like a heavy overcoat. In the jeep belonging to the Museum of Science, she let herself be rocked back and forth by the roll of the curving road, and her mood gradually turned better and better, as if she'd just gotten up.

Still clutching the viper-necktie, Aphra, the small one (I'm getting mildly tired of calling her small), kneels on the ground. With her free hand she gets her equipment out of the knapsack and lays it out neatly on a flat stone. A half-smile lingering on her finely drawn lips, she makes an incision with her scalpel in the skin behind the viper's head, lifts the tiny flap and inserts a small electronic chip. She then carefully disinfects the wound and applies a bandage two fingers wide. *The bandage will fall off in a while, it's done on purpose*, she says in that voice as clear as water, putting the viper on the ground. For an instant it is motionless, then slowly slinks off, like a patient who's been to the doctor and needs a moment to review what was said.

Daphne's now a little frightened. What if another horned viper—this rock pile seems to be full of them—suddenly appears and bites her on the ankle above her motorcycle boots? Something could go wrong. Perhaps because she sees her brow furrow, Aphra tells her it's almost impossible to get bitten by a viper; the cows Daphne has to deal with are far more dangerous. The wee one's calm is contagious and Daphne's doubts disperse like clouds racing across the sky, and disappear. Human premonitions do have a way of disappearing like that, even the accurate ones.

Leaning against a comfortable branch in a stand of larches by the side of the stone heap, Daphne observes Aphra. Her sensuous cat's body (only her head is a doe's) obviously needs to hunt this way, it's a genuine vocation for her. The horned viper is at risk of extinction and she's studying it to determine how to help save it. Watching her move, she thinks her friend is right about animal life: you have to take nature as it comes. She, instead, has always been thinking about how to modify nature, how to work out its secrets, put it on a leash, and exploit it. This new idea is slow to advance, a cart with rusty wheels, but she promises herself she'll think about it. For the moment, she's fine with this silence, with the sun that's dusting the crowns of the larch trees. Then she thinks of nothing, because she falls asleep. And sleeps like an angel (angels don't sleep, but whatever).

As they drive down toward the plain with its blotches of asphalt and concrete, Aphra says she can't bear working at the Museum of Science anymore. All they want to do is organize idiotic exhibits. Like everything else, the natural sciences are slaves to the dictatorship of the free market and the ignorance of the masses. They'll use the excuse of the recession not to hire her, they'll never give her a full-time job; she's too much of a troublemaker. But fine, she doesn't want to be complicit with a system that's driving the human race to the brink of catastrophe. She wants to farm, grow carrots and cabbages with her own hands, raise a goat and some chickens, and if possible a donkey. The time has come to organize a real resistance.

Daphne is taken aback. She's always lived in the city and can't imagine settling elsewhere. She's always believed that even the most modern agriculture is still quite backward, and must be brought up to date with technology. The wee zoologist's ideas would ordinarily horrify her, ideas so similar to the wishful thinking practiced by her mother's friend and his buddies, with their gray hair and their weakness for red wine and marijuana. And yet, when she thinks of growing carrots in semifeudal conditions, she nearly bursts into tears. She has no idea why, and she makes sure the other doesn't see her.

On their way back into town, the short one tells her she's decided to leave Vittorio. She waited for him to behave better; she's been patient, but now she's fed up. She hasn't told him yet, but she will soon, she says with gay resolve, in that tone of voice you adopt when talking about your vacation plans. Anyway, sex with him was never that great, she says, hammering in the last nail. Daphne says nothing, although she wouldn't mind talking about her two-zeros and her three-zeros, and the one-zero. Always zero. The lump in her throat has returned, and so she gazes out the side window.

THINKING OF NOTHING AGAIN

IT'S NOT THAT I'M NEGLECTING the other seven billion humans, God knows, but as will happen when one's preoccupied, I listen to them with one ear while trying to work out the problem at hand. I've never played any favorites, and honestly I'm not thrilled about starting at this venerable age. So I make an effort to do things properly, and safeguard my scrupulous, exemplary professionalism. If an old fellow is taking a long time to die, for example, I don't deliver him on the spot, as I'd be tempted to do, I let his throes go on for as long as it takes.

As soon as I can, I turn my attention back to what interests me most now (in the heat of the moment, I was about to write *the only thing*). I watch her at work in the laboratory, her white smock open over that slightly coarse skin, a blonde's skin; I watch her while she's on the toilet defecating, the blind cat on her knees; while she sleeps. I love to watch her sleep: stretched out between the sheets without the serious, thick glasses, abandoned to sleep's slightly damp and sensuous heat, her innocent sexuality smelling almost of bread, or yeast. She reminds me of one of those very long angels in certain Mannerist paintings, announcing some arrival or other, or floating on the ceiling of a church. When she's sleeping I don't fear her committing acts that offend me, and there's no danger she'll masturbate. She dreams, and I love following her optimist's dreams, fresh as the water from a brook (Petrarchan?) with continual surprises and plot twists.

It's when I watch her sleep that the craziest fantasies come to me. *My friend* (that's how I think of her in private) could become a goddess, I think. I could raise her to divine standing; that's something *the immortals* (fanciful figures beloved by the Greeks, thought to have eternal life) used to do all the time. She could become my consort. Common-law wife, concubine, whatever you like; freed, you understand, from having to expire—a fix that technically speaking is a snap. Instead of running around stealing crucifixes or stuffing herself with Sicilian cannoli, she'd be by my side, or trekking around the galaxies. She'd fit in fine: I can easily imagine her here, her and those pigtails. Instead of microbes, she'd study meteorite fragments, or some cosmic scientific enigma. There's material enough to nourish her mathematical soul for eternity, and slowly her knowledge would surpass mine (as it were). At some point she might decide to set down a giant summary bible, a compendium that would be admired to the end of time. I would no longer be alone, we'd be a couple, a pair of gods.

The present ritual foresees that God has a son, a descendant, but no consort, or companion or whatever, but you know what, the monotheistic religions would simply have to *get over it.** And I may be worrying too much; the doctrine regarding me has always been quite vague and approximate, so that married or not married wouldn't change much. Besides, there would be no need to broadcast the news to the four winds, we could just carry on discreetly for the moment. Slowly humans would begin to sniff out the fact that I was no longer alone, and then they'd have to catch up, bring the sacred texts up to date, redo the iconography and all. Taking their time.

Stop! I say to myself. *You must cease thinking about that girl this instant! Whatever happens, you must forget her. And return to thinking about nothing, which in fact is the only way to think impartially about everything! I am God!* I tell myself.

* One more proof humans are intrinsically selfish; I see no reason why they should spend their days coupling, or thinking about coupling, while I may not even take a legitimate wife.

A TERRIBLE PLANETARY INJUSTICE

ON HER ARRIVAL at the lab, everyone gazes at her the way you do someone who's just lost a close relative. But Daphne doesn't notice. She slept only about half an hour under the larch trees but feels perfectly up to carrying out the bombardment she's planned. *They seem to have posted the results of the job search*, mumbles her stoichiometric admirer, studying, as always, the shoes that stick out from under his smock, shoes a priest might wear on an outing. She listens as she would to a monumental bore, without noticing the intense glow of his phosphorescent pimples. Only after she has calmly fired off all the tiny golden bullets coated with modified genes does she go have a look. And learns that the clueless goose has won the prize. And that she has come second in the ranking. She thinks she must be dreaming, but no—she is second, and by many points. Her first thought goes to how she can save the microbe battery, the way you worry about how to protect a child.

Now as a rule the injustices of planet Earth leave me neither hot nor cold. And that's not me being cynical, but merely simple good sense. To intervene would be like trying to plug all the holes in a colander as big as the globe.* But this time I'm indignant; enough is enough. It shouldn't be terribly difficult to remedy the situation, though. I can visit a very aggressive type of leukemia on the lab director, one of those conditions that despite ample painkillers provokes harrowing screams and sends goosebumps up and down a whole hospital ward. Or better yet, I can snuff the fellow out in one go along with the charming appointee: a ceiling that collapses, a cylinder of oxygen that explodes, two souls united in job-search manipulation and in the hereafter. Now as I said, I usually abstain from such methods (so primitive), but sometimes a case needs special handling.

Finally, Daphne can't fight anymore. Fatigue descends upon her, she feels it in her stocky calves, her skinny ribs, her too-long neck, her larger-than-normal brain. She thinks she's never been so exhausted. Her colleagues try to convince her that maybe the money will turn up to renew her contract, but their words sound limp, motivated by the pity they feel for her. Even the chemist with acne seems resigned. He's crying. At this point she decides to go home.

But her bike, rather than heading back to the old fish-monger's, turns south toward the edge of town, then climbs the hills toward the flashy new villas of the nouveaux riches, and finally cuts down the scruffy valley inhabited by the leftover

---

* And mind you, (wo)men adore injustices. If I were to counter all the existing cruelties, they'd wrack their brains to come up with even more horrendous ones, even more ferocious. You can't expect a hippopotamus to walk a tightrope, or a giraffe to fly.

belligerents of 1968 and their followers. She gets to the parking lot (as it were) of her stepfather's house (as it were), removes her helmet, and realizes she has no idea what to do next. It feels like she's taken her head off. The neo-Buddhist drops the wheelbarrow he's pushing toward the hayloft—or marijuana shed—and hastens to her side. He grabs an arm to hold her up, or rather he means to, but being clumsy he trips, making things worse. She is staring straight ahead, two eyes fixed like dead orbs in a wax figure. He pushes her inside the way you push a stubborn donkey.

Now she's slumped on the broken-down sofa that the big, long-haired dog uses as a bed. The big dog is staring at his fellow canine with the short hair (who's more with it than he is) as if to ask what the hell's going on. *Why doesn't she move a muscle? Why isn't she crying?* It's like when she was three and her mother suddenly died (for her, suddenly). Recalling, perhaps, that catastrophic time, our Don Quixote look-alike observes her closely, scratching the bald part of his head. He'd like to ask her something, but they've never, ever, spoken of serious matters, so it isn't easy. But, giving his jaw a massage, he wonders aloud, what's up? *They gave it to the goose*, she replies, her voice impersonal, on automatic. Then she falls silent again, and he also says nothing.

I'm God, however, and therefore I know what his synapses are up to. He's thinking that the dapper lab director has a very fine automobile, and that these late-model vehicles make a gratifying blaze if you set fire to them, a lot of smoke and a terrible stink. Or else he could kidnap the man and stick pins in his scrotum; elite neoliberals are the worst specimens of the human race and the time has come to fight back. But then he looks at the altar with the fat fellow nude to the waist, and recalls his guru in India. It all goes toward building your karma, he thinks. Pins in the scrotum would be counterproductive.

He scratches his neck and ruminates. Some of these neoliberal sharks do deserve punishment, however, without necessarily going to extremes. A slightly less devastating version of the automotive hypothesis? He could rake the car's metallic paint job up and down with a size fifteen nail. At times the mystic spark in him does battle with an insurrectionary anarchist tendency. Before he drifted East he'd been a member of a tiny sect that urged *perpetual revolution*. But in a subsequent spiritual wave, he's decided that what happens in material life matters very little.

He brings her a beer and opens it. She drinks a sip or two, gazing at something invisible. He clears his throat loudly, the way you do when you think you have something important to say. He tells her that her mother (he calls her *Gaia*, that was her name) knew a priest who helped her when she was homeless, and with whom she used to have big discussions. He thinks Daphne ought to look him up. An imperceptible jolt runs through her, maybe just a mechanical reaction. She doesn't seem to have understood. *A guy connected with politicians and people who count, but he was also close to your mother, and he'll certainly help you out too*, he says in that unnatural voice, studying his slippers.

Daphne stares at the enigmatic layers of dirt on the floor, not seeing them. *Just you wait, you'll be able to stick with your microbes, you're so good,* says the beatnik. Finally she begins to cry, the way she cries, silently and without moving a muscle. She cries for a long time, and drinks the beer directly from the bottle, and cries. When she's done she drinks another. He hands it off to her as you do to a bike racer, and she takes it without thanks. Now another beer, still weeping in silence. Then, without being aware of it, she stretches out and falls asleep. Her "father," as he styles himself, covers her with the throw he uses for his transcendental meditation and switches off the light.

ALONE FOR A NIGHT

LAST NIGHT (as they say) while I was struggling to get to sleep (same) I thought to myself: if I were ever to try incarnation, I certainly wouldn't imitate my self-proclaimed offspring. I wouldn't go around proselytizing barefoot, or pronouncing shamanic catchphrases, as often as not false, or perform miracles. No, the appeal—I started to say the thrill—would lie in a radical transformation. No more bottomless profundity, no definitive word on things, I'd immerse myself in the partial and the finite. Do *normal things*: squeeze onto the bus at rush hour, shop in shopping centers mobbed with people, watch a TV series sprawled on a sofa. I'd sample the whole palette of human sensations: walk on an empty beach in flip-flops, hurtle down a steep slope on skis, smoke a cigarette, try a fabled Siberian sauna, board an airplane. It would be an incarnation if not quite incognito, then *private*; no trumpets, no outrageous scenes, just the dignity and composure that befit me.

The incarnation might be set in a palm grove adrift on a magnificent, transparent sea (so it looks from above, at any rate), or in a tidy Alpine village, or a bustling eastern metropolis. I'd have an *embarras du choix*, like the well-heeled tourist paging through the glossy brochures in a travel agency. And no one would prevent me from whisking myself off, free of any jet lag, should I change my mind. But I bet I'd end up settling in that ugly urban periphery that fades into the gloomy, foggy plain with its industrial fumes, its miasma of effluvia from pig- and bovine-rearing. Where Daphne lives. Those broad avenues measured out in humdrum tram stops, the resigned immigrants, the wastepaper whipped into the air by the wind: a desolate, depressing wilderness lying fallow until the real estate speculators—should the recession lift—begin building again.

And if I do decide to go for incarnation, I suppose I might as well go for fit and good-looking, rather than old. I don't mean "pretty boy"—*God save us* from bodybuilders—but not a monster either. A young fellow with all his hair, a pleasing and trustworthy face, a well-turned body, and the toned and well-proportioned reproductive apparatus of a Greek statue.* I wouldn't mind eyeglasses; I've always found them alluring. Of course there's no reason I couldn't be a girl, although maybe I'd feel a bit (I worry here about being accused of sexist bigotry) like a transvestite.

---

* Physical appearance has always had an exaggerated importance for the humans, according to them for reasons linked to so-called "evolution." By choosing attractive mates the women hope to produce strapping young offspring. The men are likewise convinced that a pleasing appearance will guarantee against disease and frailty. It's difficult to see why, now that they've cleverly found ways around mere evolution, good looks should count even more.

If I wished, I could be incarnated as a billionaire rolling in luxury and privilege; the effort (*effort?*) involved would be the same. But the truth is, I would rather be incarnated as a very normal person. I've never liked rich people; ninety-nine times out of a hundred they consider themselves superior to the rest simply because they possess a few more things, and they expect the world to worship at their feet. On this point I'm in agreement with my son, although some of his extreme positions leave me puzzled, to say the least.*

Once I appeared in man form, I wonder what my very first action, my *baptism*, if you will, would be. Would I down an espresso standing at the bar, studying the other customers over the rim of the cup? Take an elevator? How would I behave with Daphne, supposing I were to run across her? Would I dare to speak of my feelings, if they are feelings? And if she gave me the brush-off, what would I do—I who am accustomed to always getting whatever I want? Who can guarantee (I'm now trying to look at this from the human angle) that she wouldn't mistreat me like she does the silent chemist, as women so often do? How would I deal with being reduced to hopeless yearning, losing my appetite, becoming a wreck? Wouldn't I take it pretty badly?

The most disturbing (put it that way) thing is to recognize that in some ways I might like it, being in despair. Looking

---

* I sometimes think that if he were to come back in these times when money has become sacred, he would be a terrorist. No more turning the other cheek to receive a fresh kick in the backside.

down from the top of a skyscraper, one can feel drawn to the abyss below. I mean just for a moment, just enough to understand what it means to feel a hard lump in your throat, a weight on your chest, eyes smarting. To have no future ahead, only *a desert of unhappiness.*

HIDDEN SECURITY CAMS

AS SHE TAKES THE STAIRS of the Stock Breeders' Association three at a time, Daphne decides she'll profit from this unexpected convocation to ask the president for the go-ahead to do more inseminations, not that she's in favor of the procedure any more now than she was before—if anything, the more she thinks about it, she's opposed—but it's better than nothing when you need work. Striding up to the desk of the secretary who reminds her of Cleopatra, she sees the woman staring at her outfit as if the punk look annoys her even more than usual. There's a gleam of triumph in her eye, too, a joy greedy for warm blood, then her glance is rerouted to the tumid cactus next to the photograph of her family.

Daphne shrugs this off with a horsey shake of her long neck and enters the presidential office. The man, stout with tiny round eyes, usually beams her one of those crude testosteronic smiles he aims at all young women whether pretty or not, lust pretending to be amiable good humor. Today, though, he welcomes her chin up, his bull's head tilted to one side, arms crossed, barricaded behind his desk. Before addressing a word to her, he searches for something on the computer. But he can't find it. He snorts; he's like a bull waiting for the bullfight to begin, she thinks. Bulls have trouble distinguishing real cows from imitations; imagine how they do with computers. And his fingers are too fat; he needs a large keyboard like on those children's games.

Finally the president nods, that head of his grafted to a bull's neck bobs up and down. He's found what he was looking for. A few seconds of private jubilation and then he turns the flat screen toward her, making a *ladies and gentlemen, may I present* semicircle with his arm that could be mistaken for humor but ends in a violent jerk. On the screen, a blue and white video from a security camera, showing an empty, darkish corridor, no one present. For quite a while absolutely nothing happens apart from the quivering of the poor-quality image. There's only the corridor, and that queasy, empty feeling of nothing happening (redundant phrase meant to make the account more gripping). Then a door opens, slowly, and she steps out. It would be difficult to mistake her; she's wearing the leather jacket she has on right now under her worker's overalls, and her motorcycle boots are identical, not to mention the unmistakable sideways braidlets. She strides out confidently and enters another door at the opposite corner of the image. A few moments later she reappears with a crucifix in hand, holding it tightly in her fist like a hatchet. Now standing before the door she first came out of, she places the object in her rucksack, the same that's now sitting at her feet. Like a fisherman carefully depositing the fish he's just fished. Then she disappears, and the door closes behind her.

Without any interruption, another video begins playing. We see a hall with many rows of chairs and a pulpit supplied with a microphone at the far end. An oblique light enters through picture windows on one side, as if it were a summer evening. Or an August afternoon. Daphne remembers everything. It was the Catholic summer camp next to the huge, newly renovated stable that belongs to the Curia, not far from the lakeshore with those monumental musty old villas. She had just finished work and had thought, while I'm here, how about a spot of hunting? And just then she appears, looking behind her as if she's heard something. At the back of the pulpit, she reaches up for the crucifix on the wall above. But it's too high up; even on tiptoe and stretching to the max, she can't reach it. Now she goes to get a chair and stands on it, detaching my so-called son from the wall and, without getting down from the chair, she studies the figure up close. Suddenly she dashes it to the floor, furious.

For some time now manufacturers in certain parts of Asia have been able to imitate wood perfectly, and at rock-bottom prices. But plastic crosses cannot be burned in wood stoves. There's your problem. The president can't know that, however, he simply thinks she's deranged. He watches her over the top of the screen, on his feet now, as if she were a ruthless Islamic terrorist. Absurd, she's never murdered anyone: in the video she leans over and carefully collects the splintered pieces of

Christ and his cross. You can't see all the details in the flickering images; she's hunkered down on the floor. Seen from the back, she looks as if she might be peeing. She remembers the moment; she swept up all the Christian fragments and put them in her pocket.

Now the president turns the screen back around so it faces the herd of bovines and the sunset out the window, exhaling from his nose, himself a bull collecting his thoughts. He stares at her without saying a word. At long last he's free to express all the male chauvinist disapproval he harbors, which, mixed as it is with sexual desire, is formidable and highly impulsive. *There are at least a couple of actionable offenses here*, he declares. *Breaking and entering and burglary*, he says, counting on his enormous fingers. She thinks she may faint. Nothing like this has happened to her for what feels like a lifetime. This sensation of being at the mercy of the enemy, at risk of being annihilated, she first encountered when she went to the nuns' boarding school/prison in elementary and middle school. By high school she had learned how to use her scholastic achievements as a defense weapon.

Not even a mentally deranged person would consider stealing crucifixes, says the Minotaur. The more he thinks about it, the more enraged he seems. In fact he's not a practicing Catholic and even less a believer, and never mind about the details of his so-called private life. Still, the more indignant he acts, the more indignant he becomes. He scuttles across the office and back, his pacing indignant, his nostrils bristling with outrage, and all his pores too. *What shall we do then? Shall I call the police or the carabinieri?* he says, staring fiercely at the telephone on his desk. He seems to think he's on a stage.

The beanpole is unable to say a word, she's drenched in cold sweat. She would like to signal no with her head, but she's paralyzed. It isn't just shame, but the sensation she's being totally crushed, physically and morally. Her ever-efficient brain tells her that soon the carabinieri—only a fool would think this is a matter for the police—will arrive and drag her down to the station. They'll search the old fishmonger's and find the big woven plastic sacks full to the brim with stolen goods. All those dozens of friars and parish priests who have filed suit to get their lost St. Josephs or Three Kings back will rub their hands with glee and demands for compensation will rain on her head like confetti. And then they'll find her computer and discover the secret data she's hacked into. The news will make the papers: *Crucifix- and Virgin-burglar arrested; search of her home computer turns up top secret Vatican documents.* When she gets out of prison she'll be sleeping on the street, wheeling around town with a supermarket cart full of rags. And right now there is nothing she can do to get herself off the hook.*

---

* One of the great problems non-believers face, when push comes to shove, is that there's no one to turn to. Reason and Science never came to anyone's aid in a pinch. And why should they?

A TITANIC STRUGGLE WITH MYSELF

I'VE BEEN THINKING about it, and I've come to a decision. This has to stop. Without of course all the drama and tear-jerking that a human being would indulge in if (s)he were in my place. This is a titanic struggle; in some ways I'm like a volcano ready to erupt—but there must be no thunder and lightning, no earthquakes and whirlwinds to blow off steam, no massacres of innocents. A god shows his mettle even in the most difficult circumstances, indeed above all in the most difficult circumstances. *I am God*, as I say.

To cancel the lanky one from my thoughts and be just God, period, seems to me the most merciless sentence imaginable, the cruelest. A fate worse than that recent asteroid in free fall, worse than a helpless guppy about to be devoured by a bigger fish, gobbled up in turn by a bigger. But I have a plan. I'm smitten, I couldn't be more smitten, but I've decided, and when a god decides, we're done.

I've decided I'll help her, then return to being Me. It's not my place to play the algorithm for an online dating site, but I'm going to find her a boyfriend. Indeed, I'll show my divine magnanimity by finding her a guy who's close to perfect: attentive, accommodating, easygoing, simpatico. A guy who's not obsessed with sex, who doesn't think of that and only that, unlike the climatologist. A lad who feels the desire to couple from time to time, like a normal human being, and is even capable of respecting that commandment about thy neighbor's wife.

They'll meet *by chance* and discover they're *made for each other*. Ka-pow! *Love at first sight*. It will be the just conclusion of this business, the only outcome that's suited to my status. But first I have to take care of all the side issues. One thing at a time. There's no big hurry for this boyfriend, right?

The hunky Vittorio has already been dispatched to the land of kangaroos and descendants of British pickpockets. I arranged for his eye to fall on an ad for a job at an Australian university; they were looking for a research professor with just his profile. On a lark—the salary was *unbelievable*—he sent off an application, never dropping his usual ironic nonchalance. The reply came right back: he was just the person they were looking for. Due to *unforeseen circumstances* a certain project had been seriously delayed and so they were in a hurry.

After he'd read over the compensation clause of the contract five or six times, not a whiff of his dopaminic ardor for Daphne persisted. The fickleness of men never fails to amaze me. He didn't even go over to wish her farewell in person, the miserable cad; he just sent a shower of faux-comical text messages. I was tempted to mete out some small, suitable punishment, but instead I helped him with his preparations, and I even put his elbow right—in two days it was working like new—to facilitate his departure. And thus he and his irresistible smile did really take off, and on the airplane he made friends with a Tyrolean damsel wearing a push-up bra and a Pentecost-purple headset. Sorry, but from now on, this diary will feature one character less, and you'll have to make do with the ones who are left.

THE REGISTERED LETTER
WITH MANY STAMPS

THE MINOTAUR picks up the phone and slowly dials three digits. *Police*, thinks Daphne, who isn't at all surprised he's made the stupid choice. While he waits he's drumming his Picassian fingers on the desk as he readies himself to explain the situation. He's still waiting. Then suddenly he puts the phone down, as if seized by a raptus. *Okay, I'm not going to pursue this, but don't you ever set foot in here again*, he shouts, waving his arms as if she's an annoying animal to be chased away. *Out!* he screams. *And don't think you'll ever work as an inseminator again*, he yells at her back as she grabs the door handle, as if the thought had just occurred to him. *Not even in Basilicata!*

When the secretary with the heels and the Byzantine-Egyptian prostitute makeup sees her appear, she trains her triumphant eyes on her, she too playing the defender of the Catholic faith. When in fact for the past two years and two months—if we want to dot our I's and cross our T's—she's been indulging in adulterous afternoon sex on the presidential armchair. That's a fact that the beanpole would never suss out even in normal conditions, however, and certainly not today.

Back on the street without knowing how and why she got there, she feels like she's drunk. She's crying without knowing she's crying. I must admit that I, too, am somewhat upset. Of course I knew about the security cameras that recorded her stealing the crucifixes, I knew that's why she'd been called in, and I even knew he'd put the phone down without talking to the law. But it's one thing to know what's going to happen, another to *witness* it happening, as it were, *in first person*. Feelings can confuse you. I was almost expecting the police to answer the phone and send over a patrol. And right now I almost have a lump in my throat watching her weep like that. Omnipotence: it also means having a lump in your throat without having a throat.

As she parks her bike in front of the old fishmonger's, she thinks that at least she has a place to live, and that's something. Recession or no recession, she'll find a way to make a little money. It was never going to last, that insemination gig; what happened was bound to happen. In short, she tells herself some baseless encouraging lies, the way humans do to boost their spirits.

Poking out of the mailbox is a registered letter plastered with many stamps; it seems the Indian signed for it in her absence (and here I'm putting myself in her shoes; this is merely a hypothesis). She opens it thinking it must be some receipt for tax purposes, and finds that the owner of the fishmonger's has written to say her lease will not be extended.

The place is going to be renovated and she must vacate in two months. She has to read the words three or four times before they penetrate her brain, and it dawns on her that this is an eviction notice. Now she begins to cry again. She sobs sitting on the toilet, and the blind cat on her knees wonders what heaven those salty drops come from and what that metrical braying's supposed to mean.

I'LL BE MUTE AS A FISH

I WISH I COULD tell her that she can relax. Job, housing, love, leisure time: I'm going to put it all right. I'll come up with an apartment that's not very expensive to rent but *nice*, with a proper, *God-given* (pardon my word play) bed. And if all goes well (it will!) she'll be able to pursue that research of hers she's so thrilled about. *No worries, Daphne, I'll take care of everything*, I'd like to tell her. *I'm here—you know, God*, I'd like to whisper in her ear, tenderly but reassuringly.

But instead I remain mute as a fish, true to my habitual divine reserve. No matter what happens, no matter how bad the mess she's in. It pains me to see her like this, but I can't let myself be taken hostage by sentiment or act out of impulse. There's a time for everything. This evening I'll limit myself to sending her a proper restorative sleep to enjoy in her dry aquarium. Sleep is important when things go badly, otherwise the nerves (I won't go into the technical details) become exhausted. I'm also supervising her dreams personally; to cheer her up, some charming Zeffirellian romantic nonsense in pastel colors with Florentine embellishments—and a few baroque Greenaway strokes here and there. Not exactly her style, but it should do the trick.

Of course, atheist that she is, when she sees that her problems have been resolved, she'll think things worked out all by themselves. She'll say she was *super lucky*, after all that *had shit* (her terminology) that befell her. I don't mind. To love means to be concerned with the welfare of the beloved person above all, not with one's own (and this tale is taking me where it wants to go).

SUPERMARKET CHECKOUT CLERK

SHE TOLD HERSELF that standing in front of the supermarket register wouldn't be especially tiring. But in fact, she realized right away that time in that consumer prison was mired in a stomach-turning swamp of baked ham, laundry detergent, pecorino cheese and aftershave. Time had stopped. Her colleagues told her that she'd get used to it, but she's convinced she'll die before that moment comes. Every day is an unending torture. She's so wiped out in the evening that her head feels like it's made of many tiny pieces badly glued together, pieces that themselves are tagged for sale. And the final blow is that to get home now, she has to take the subway first and then a bus. One morning she'd left the house and found that her beautiful twin-cylinder was gone. Well, there was a piece of the lock, which they'd managed to force. The chain, they made off with.

The first days she glanced at the shoppers' bodies and faces. It's incredible how much you can determine about a human being from a lightning glance, she would think, back then when she was still enjoying developing theories, translating this thing into mathematical and IT terms. But then she realized that classifying faces and clothing was just one more effort on top of the effort of having to smile. It was better just to keep her head down and restrict her movements to what was necessary to push the products by and take the cash or card. Now she behaves like the others, she spares herself.

After just a couple of weeks, the clientele now rolls by one after the other like silhouettes of refugees, clots of stress made of flesh and odors, but mostly of a great deal of anxiety, of angst. Nearly all are in a foul humor, or a hurry,* and she doesn't need to look at them to know that, she can feel it in her sternum. At peak hours the queue in front of her register grows longer. Supermarkets aren't happy places; people leave their happiness outside in hopes they'll find it later in the things they've put in their cart, each with its penitentiary barcode.

If she knew this was just a temporary situation, she'd be taking it better, poor thing. But the unemployment rate has been worsening, and in her deterministic mind that means she'll be tied to that *shitty register* (her words) for eternity. I've stopped sending her signals of hope; numbskull that she is, she doesn't pick up on them. I arranged for her to meet a fortune-teller in the subway who predicted she would resume

---

* If there's any church that reveals how badly off human beings are, now that they've rid themselves of Me, it's the supermarket; I can't disagree with her.

her research on bacteria-fueled energy. She thought the woman had simply guessed her job *by chance*. I made sure she saw a horoscope announcing splendid times to come for Sagittarians of the Third Decade. She laughed bitterly, that big mouth of hers spreading even wider. She won't believe it until she can reach out a hand and touch it, the materialist.

As you can imagine, I could find her another job if I really wanted to, never mind the recession. But this is the path I've chosen. Many novices think a god reasons like a traffic cop, but with all due respect for traffic cops, a god's actions are lofty and very complex. Above all, a god has to keep in mind the welfare of millions and millions of believers, billions of believers, foreseeing their infinite interactions and giving priority to those who deserve it, the faithful of the faithful, as is only right. If it was just a question of looking after one person, a monad untouched by gravity, floating in some sterile no-man's-land, anyone could do it.

By now her movements are automatic. She slides the products by the barcode reader in one continuous motion, but not too fast: she must look efficient but not exhaust herself before the eight hours are up. She knows the supervisor with the belly that makes him look pregnant is watching her from his elevated booth; he picked her out as snooty right away, reading the puzzled looks of a nearsighted mathematician as contempt. She can't see him through the reflections on the glass, but he is staring at particular sections of her body with his lewd watery cow's eyes. I can't help it if all her bosses lust after her and bother her the way a satyr bothers a wood nymph; I merely report the situation. In theory, there are supposed to be persons of both sexes at the registers, but in fact the ones working there are all female and all have ample backsides and thighs. Those are the tastes of Cerberus the Expectant.

MAN'S EXISTENCE

I NEVER REALLY UNDERSTOOD how tragic (wo)man's existence is until I saw it up close. Humans are constantly at the mercy of all sorts of illnesses, accidents, and environmental catastrophes; from one minute to the next their situation can go from tolerable to utterly untenable. The only thing for certain is that they must die, usually in dreadful pain: not a very cheering certainty. In such conditions, it's pointless for them to make plans for the future, but they keep on making them anyway, they never give up.

Once I considered them awful whiners, chronic depressives, inveterate grudge-holders. Now I think I understand them, somewhat. It can't be pleasant to be hungry, terribly hungry, and then when you do find something to eat, you get a stomachache because you ate too much. To be cold, terribly cold, and dream of being in a warm place, then a split second later find you're dying of the heat and longing for it to be cool. To desire a partner and suffer atrocious heartache because the other's keeping you at arm's length, then to realize that you're bored to death with that person and tempted to commit murder. To observe the relentless furrowing of your own skin, the deterioration of your vital organs, and know that your brain, too, is beginning to fail.

Humans, incapable of being happy, spend their entire existence fantasizing they will be happy in the future. Five minutes later, half an hour later, that afternoon, next year, ten years hence, all the hitches and the problems will vanish, the desired state will materialize out of nothing and *as if by magic* everything will be easy, jolly. Unlike the other animals they are born premature, and no matter how hard they try they can never catch up; something about them always remains infantile, unfinished.* They try to make up for this by telling a million stories, twisting the facts, philosophizing, drowning in their own words. All vain efforts; unhappy they are, unhappy they remain.

Maybe I should have inverted the life cycle, putting death at the beginning of their existence and birth at the end. It might be a relief to them to be done with the perishing—*out with the tooth, out with the pain*—and have the icing on the cake ahead of them: a peaceful, delightful childhood. Maybe that way their condition would seem more acceptable, and they'd be happier. The intolerable stages of maturity and senescence finished, they would slip into a pleasant unconsciousness, running around, playing and screaming like children. And then they'd re-enter their mothers' wombs without suffering

---

* They even project this shortcoming of theirs on yours truly; it's just impossible to have a mature relationship with them.

and without regret, the way you park a car in the garage at night, to enjoy life's one period of genuine tranquility and fusion with the universe. Eight to nine months and they'd be back to the embryonic stage, then just a rowdy spermatozoon or an ovum, and then nothing.

THE CARROTS
AND THE HOE

IT'S ONLY 6 P.M. and she'd give anything to be able to escape right now, or even just lock herself in the bathroom. What heaven it would be to sit on the toilet and smoke a cigarette; it's forbidden, but she's been doing it anyway. Today, between one shopper and another, she hasn't even had time to take a deep breath. What's worse, she thinks the stink of the supermarket, the gorgonzola and the hair spray and all that, must have permeated her bronchial tubes, her flesh, and her skin. Every time she looks at the clock next to the pregnant ogre's booth, she finds only a minute has passed, or at the best, two. Time stands still in this quagmire she's fallen into.

When she's finished she heads for the wee one's house, although she's a wreck and wouldn't mind going straight home. But they said they'd meet. The one-bedroom/zoo is in turmoil; Aphra seems very pleased to see her but every few seconds her phone rings anew and she's going on about banners, frontiers to cross, the van they'll be traveling in and possible police roadblocks. The cockatoo and the other animals seem worried. Is she about to get into some kind of trouble again? When she was in prison before, the household had descended into chaos. As if replying to their concerns, she explains she's taking off for a little town in eastern Europe where they plan to mow down a field of genetically modified corn and dump it in the town square. And then they'll liberate 2,000 pigs from a giant pen where they're given only genetically modified feed. She's leaving early tomorrow morning.

While she boils water to make tea, she speaks of Vittorio. Smiling as always, her big eyes slightly droopy, she tells Daphne that he's had some *awesome freakin' luck* (I merely report what she said); *as things turned out* he's now doing exactly what he wanted to and making a *shitload of money*. She's really happy for him, she says, her cheeks trembling. Really happy, she says again, rubbing her eyes. She begins to cry. Her face crumples up like a baby, and her sobs are accompanied by high-pitched throaty yelps. The phone rings again but she doesn't answer. Maybe she doesn't even hear it. Daphne wraps a long arm around her shoulder, she too quite teary. She's crying, you understand, also and maybe primarily on her own behalf, as humans always do.

Truth is, Aphra's happy that Vittorio is ten thousand miles away, she tells Daphne when she's calmed down a bit and is stroking the other's back. Although she's in the dumps right now. The cockatoo is back on her shoulder; he seems to want to be sure to hear what she's saying. It was the last thing she'd expected,* she goes on, patting her long Bambi eyelashes dry. Then she cries some more, but smiling to show her impish teeth. The telephone rings again and this time she answers. Cocò, the prying white cockatoo, takes off and lands on the refrigerator, his high-strung head-wagging a signal the tragedy is over.

What we could do is rent some land, the two of us, she pipes up. *A house to live in and a nice piece of land to cultivate,* she adds, patting the fox cub with the injured leg that's climbed onto her lap. (Cocò is observing them suspiciously from atop the fridge.) Daphne freezes, her teacup at half-mast. She has always detested rural silence, broken only by the chickens clucking and the hum of the neighbor's tractor, rows of crops as far as the eye can see. *What a great idea,* says her mouth, however. And now that she's said it, she really does think she'd like to live out in the country with her friend, indeed it seems to be the only way to rid herself of the supermarket. She feels tremendously relieved, thinking of it.

Aphra's eyes caress her, bright with yearning. You're so intelligent, she tells Daphne, it's obvious you'll invent a ton of new ways to irrigate the crops and to preserve them. *When are you going to take me to meet your stepfather?* she continues without waiting for any comment from the other. *I really want to see that place of his and talk to him,* she says, pressing her palms together. At this point her eyes are open wide, transfixed.

---

* If I may, her reaction is just one more example of the utter inconsistency of human beings. They want something, and when they get it, they complain.

Daphne promises to take her there, but she thinks privately that she never will; her friend would be terribly disappointed by that loser ex-friend of her mother and the pigsty he lives in, that junkyard. Anyway, he'd be struck dumb as he always is; it would just be embarrassing. She can't figure out where the little one got that bee in her bonnet.

Nor does the prospect of hoeing fields of carrots seem that appealing, she thinks as she heads toward the subway stop in the freezing rain. She and her friend are just hardwired to be incompatible, it seems: that little bombshell of energy and good humor has her own battles to fight, her vegan friends, her neo-rustic dreams. She's into animism, and the animals she looks after and their souls—to her mind they have souls, something like powerful computers. She dreams of a world where everyone grows carrots and they hold public meetings to decide everything. Daphne, instead, beyond her blind, nymphomaniac cat, has nothing. No family, no orgasms, not even, ultimately, any principles to defend. She's not even sure whether she's for or against genetically modified organisms, she's not sure of anything. She just knows she's unhappy, and that the only thing she's really good at is being unhappy.

It breaks my heart (figure of speech) to see her in this state. Of course I had the bus come right away and made sure she found a seat even though it was crowded. *Take it easy, your bike will soon turn up*, I wish I could say to her. *And little by little all the rest will be resolved too, my sweetheart (my sweetheart!)* But no, I'm mute as a fish. *I am God*, I tell myself. *God.*

THE ANGELIC INDIAN
FROM PARADISE

THERE'S A KNOCK at the door of the old fishmonger's, and Daphne, her spirits lower than her shoes, drags herself across to open up, convinced it will be the only person who ever stops by without telephoning first. And in fact, it is an Indian. But he's younger than the fellow next door, and better looking. Actually, he's gorgeous: two large coal-black eyes; wavy gleaming dark hair with a petroleum shine; smooth, luminous skin over cheekbones that are expressive but gentle; elegant, almost violet-colored lips that seem to be drawn with a single, very fine stroke of the pen; the whitest teeth, sparkling with saliva; a beautiful neck, beautiful clavicles, beautiful wrists, beautiful hands. *I am the cousin of your neighbor*, he says, his angel's hand pressing his chest. She says nothing, overwhelmed by this unexpected masculine annunciation; for a moment she truly thinks she sees something glowing around his head. *We need a cable to connect the computer to the printer, would you be able to lend us one?* the angel goes on, as if reading her mind, and almost excusing himself. He traces a cable in the air, arms as light as a dancer, or maybe a funambulist, maybe a bit ironic and with a melancholy grace.

I'm Aryaman, he says, holding out a hand as smooth and cool as a bolt of silk. His smile is the smile of an irresistibly friendly and appealing angel, a secular angel (I put myself in her shoes). Not even his voice seems earthly; it's as enchanting as a baroque cantata (my comparison this time). Daphne's mouth hangs open; so much beauty is disturbing, outrageous. She's certain this apparition hasn't appeared by chance; he's the one she's been waiting for a long time, forever. *It's him.* I watch the words pop up in her left cerebral cortex, like huge red letters suddenly appearing on a screen.

She invites him in, a steadfast smile on her face, euphoric, unmindful of the mess. He, too, seems to pay no attention to the graveyard of dead soda cans and the plates of decomposing leftovers that fill the room. It's clear his thoughts soar very high, despite two magnificent feet shaped like slender dugouts that are firmly planted on the ground. He sits down on the polystyrene-chip sofa; she asks if he'd like tea, and he, extending his swan's neck forward, says *yes*. She fills a pan with water and takes the teapot out of the chest full of crockery. But then, rather than light the burner, she grabs two large tumblers, pours in rum, adds some ice cubes, some liquid cane sugar and a squeeze of lemon. Then some pineapple segments that were in her electric cooler, and some cinnamon. And a mint leaf. She walks toward him, wagging her forefinger in the air to say *wait, I had a better idea.*

The angel stares at the tumbler, a very fine line snaking across his faultless, very lofty brow. You might almost think it was the first time he'd ever held a glass of rum in his hand. As if he is wondering how the devil his cherubic body will take to this earthly substance. He sniffs it and drinks a minuscule sip. *Excellent*, he says (and he means it). He seems delighted to be there, seems to have forgotten all about the printer cable. He gazes at her the way you might some delicious dessert, but his anthracite eyes are also full of admiration, if slightly abashed by his secret appetites.

My cousin tells me you're pretty good with the computer, he says in a fluty voice. *I understand you can find your way into any network*. His delicious, slightly lopsided smile hints at IT skills and connivance. *Once I was able to take down a large bank for a couple of hours*, he adds, lifting his shoulders. She's been concentrating on the Vatican site this year, Daphne tells him; it's one of the most impregnable strongholds there is. It took her an age, but she was finally able to hack into the banking system and she's also downloaded a bunch of reports from a top-secret investigation of pedophilia. Now she wants to publicize them, but she hasn't figured out how to go about it yet.

She doesn't have a clue why she's blabbing about such matters to this stranger; she hasn't even told Aphra about the big flaw she discovered in the Vatican software, or the secret reports. Well, actually she does have a clue; she's certain that this angel—even atheists are awed by angels—is the soul mate she's been awaiting for years, forever. She knew it from the minute she saw him, she knew he'd been sent by magic. That's why her heart is pounding like an African war drum, and at the same time she feels terribly calm, with that peace of mind that accompanies solemn moments and important decisions. She's finally met *the man of her life*.

Daphne looks at him and he looks at her, as when the conversation is about to undergo a change of topic. Instead, and without consulting her brain, she stretches out her long neck in his direction, and he, at the same time, moves his head toward hers. They suddenly find their mouths glued together as if the matter had been decided long ago. Taking possession of those hard, violet lips that taste faintly of bay leaves, she greedily drinks in other hints of incense and deep stellar space; he seems to like the vanilla-and-lightly-oxidized-copper flavor of her tongue. They drink in each other's breath and exchange saliva. The boyish Indian is very grave; he seems to savor every least sensation with a surgeon's concentration. It's almost as if he were touching a woman for the first time.

After a long appetizer of feverish kissing and touching, Daphne drags him confidently to her bed. He sinks into the fish tank, a kind of rough baptism. In no time they are half naked and she opens her legs for him. The speed of it all rather stuns him, maybe even intimidates; he doesn't seem quite sure what to do next. However, he takes his courage in two hands and propels it stiffly toward her abdomen. Everything seems to suggest a long amorous skirmish, but then his pelvis suddenly jerks forward and he's taken by violent shivers. He looks down, shocked, two long furrows lining his brow; he's devastated, trying to understand. He can't take it in; he's terribly embarrassed.

Daphne, when she understands what's happened, begins to laugh. The more downcast he looks, the more she laughs uncontrollably. For her, the thing isn't serious at all, it's a gas. She wets her hand with his angelic sperm, and still laughing, spreads it on her thighs and belly. With her index finger she paints three lines across her forehead, and dots the lobes of both ears. Now he laughs too, not entirely willingly. She understands it's better not to make too much of it, and begins to caress his head, his fine, very black hair. She kisses his neck and his lovely neatly shaped Indian nose. *Sorry*, she whispers between one kiss and another. *Afterwards you get another chance*, she says. It's not easy not to laugh, but she's determined to control herself.

They begin to kiss and touch each other as before. He's smiling now, but his breathing is a bit odd, like a dog when it's terribly thirsty. Or as if he's had a great fright, or is still fearful of something. She makes every effort to put him at his ease. She's not worried; she's known cases like this and they usually resolve themselves in no time at all. She kisses him all over, and touches his private parts very expertly. But he's terribly awkward. He's as gorgeous as the sun itself, and his head with its glints of petroleum seems to glow with a halo of purest light. But his body is as tense as a steel cable holding up a suspension bridge. And he's not smiling anymore. He doesn't want to look like a fool, but his member is just not getting hard. And he doesn't think it will get hard later, and the more he thinks about it, the more unlikely it seems it ever will. This is why he feels bad. He'd like to be able to say *Stand to attention right now*, as a god could. But he is merely a normal human being.

He's young, full of energy, he knows he's very attractive, he wants that girl above all things, but for some reason his member just lies there shriveled up like a punctured football. It doesn't want to harden, not even a little. This is why he's so ill at ease, why the cold sweat. He never dreamed something like this could happen. He'd like to be somewhere deep underground, not in that fish tank made into a bed. Daphne tries again to rouse him, she changes position and takes him in her mouth, cupping his testicles in one hand and poking her naughty fingers between his buttocks—a recipe that's usually infallible. The Hellenic member remains limp, while Aryaman has become a marble statue, his expression a baroque wince of pain. It's beautiful, like everything about him, but still a mask of suffering. It's clear he just wants to die. She switches out of sex mode, and draws him close, pats his back and his head to make him understand that it's nothing serious. Actually, the thing makes her feel even more tender about him. And above all, she loves lying next to that beautiful body as night begins to fall. It makes her happy.

Soon she's asleep. It's a very deep and slightly unnatural sleep: an immersion in the abyss of anesthesia, or a voyage to Hades. When she wakes it's totally dark outside and there's no one by her side. She sits up and leans over the edge of the tank to look around, but the Indian isn't there. The events of the day pass through her mind, but as if they had taken place a long time ago, and the contours are vague. She tries to focus, asking herself how that heavenly young man could have known of her hacking activities, given that she'd never talked to anyone about them, and certainly not her neighbor. That too is very strange. But it was no dream: there's a large stain on the sheet that's still not entirely dry. She sniffs it: yep, it's semen. And there are two empty glasses in front of the sofa. The printer cable is still looped over the back of the chair with the legs sawed off.

The following afternoon when she returns from the supermarket she stops by her neighbor's, and as always he receives her with heartrending smiles, patting the palms of his hands together like a man applauding. Her throat caught in a noose, she asks if his cousin is still staying there. He stares at her, blinking his deep-set eyes in their dark orbits; he doesn't understand. Articulating her words carefully, she explains that she met his cousin the day before; he came by to ask for a printer cable, and she wanted to know if they had solved the problem. He continues to smile very politely, but he still doesn't understand, if anything he understands less. *Your cousin*, she says, pointing a finger at him and looking around. *I have many cousins, but they are not here*, he says, pleased to have finally grasped what she's saying.

Okay, but yesterday afternoon your cousin came by to ask me for a printer cable, she says again, arms miming a printer and a cable. She thinks she may be going crazy. Her body seems to be leaving her, it seems to be turning to dry wood. With his usual delicious Hindu politeness, but also very firmly, he repeats that none of his cousins are in the vicinity. *Maybe next year my cousin comes*, he says, waving a hand to make it clear it's still not certain. This time he doesn't smile, he seems unhappy to disappoint her. She apologizes and drags her wooden legs over to the old fishmonger's, looking around for some proof that yesterday's otherworldly encounter indeed took place. But she had washed the glasses before going off to the supermarket and cleaned up in the hopes the celestial Indian would return. There are no other signs of his supernatural apparition. She goes to look at the sheet, but the stain is no more. She inspects it inch by inch passing the fabric between her hands, but no stain is to be found. By *some strange set of circumstances (set of circumstances!)* it disappeared when it dried out. Just evaporated. She hunkers down on the floor and begins to cry, and the blind cat leaps onto her knees, muttering in the furtive but high-strung language of cats that yes, it is a bad, bad moment.

EXTERMINATE THE THOUGHTS

I'VE HIT ROCK BOTTOM. It's language that reduced me to this state, it's the agitating, incitement-to-riot effect of the written word and the smokescreen of uncontrolled feelings that words belch out, as the fire grows more and more enraged with each bucket of gasoline tossed on it. Every language contains all the folly that humans are capable of; language just spills it from their mouths. It makes no difference whether it's coming from the oral cavity of a god or of the last clandestine migrant to arrive; the important thing so far as language is concerned is to foment, to befoul, to devastate. You write one sentence and you toss on the first bucket of gasoline, immediately the flames of hyperbole and intolerable grief flare up, and the more you write, the crazier you get, the more you're convinced you believe what you've said, the more you're on your way to pure madness, to plotting nefarious plots. Whereas if you never think, or worse, write, you won't have moods or feelings, and you can live blissfully and serenely for billions of years. With no risk of screwing up.

The problems arise with the very first thought, whatever

it is. Because that first damn thought will immediately invite another, which will be: *Am I right to think that?* Not to mention the third, which will almost certainly contradict the first, without, however, dismissing the second. And the fourth will be *Why do I exist?* and the fifth, *Do I really exist?* and the sixth, *Am I in love?* and so forth and so on, and all the while you're behaving ever more inappropriately, ever more rashly. Thoughts are infectious, they contaminate actions, they create monsters.

Millions of human beings would cheat and steal to have even a millionth of my powers and my privileges, I know. They'd think this business (*business!*) involving the ex-inseminatrix with the purple braids is a non-event, insignificant. *Nobody ever died of love!* they'd say. *He'll get over it like everyone else gets over it!* Of course, they're all convinced that if they were in my shoes they'd fare better than I. I'm getting mighty tired of this arrogance of theirs. Ever since my supposed son persuaded them I'm a harmless social worker, if not actually an old fool, I've had to listen to their sermons.

Everything would be simpler if I could just take off on a trip, some hike or safari to rest my brain and empty out everything to do with that woman. Or even if I could retire for a while to an isolated galaxy where omniscience and omni-foresight were out of order, like those places where there's no phone signal. I'd concentrate solely and exclusively on my own affairs. *Out of sight, out of mind*, as the notorious proverb goes. But there's no way I can run off somewhere else or look the other way: wherever I turn I see her, wherever I go, she's there. Not to mention that my memory is perpetually infallible.

What men have going for them is that they forget; little by little they forget everything. All those broken hearts capable of fastening onto substitute love objects in a flash; all those inconsolable widows who one day start to dance and flirt again. And then of course they die, and that's the most radical type of oblivion there is. While I never forget and I don't die. I can fool myself for an instant thinking about something else, but one part of my mammoth brain never lets go of the bone. And anyone who comes up with a better metaphor here, please let me know.*

It's easy to vow to do something, harder to get down to business without hesitating or changing one's mind, even though in my case we're dealing with metaphysical facts (if I may be permitted an oxymoron). I knew very well what I must not do, knew that I mustn't allow myself to be tempted, and yet something went awry. The only solution at this point is to close up shop—mental shop I mean, exterminating those thoughts before they see the light of day. So that everything can return to normal. And I'll recall these events as a terrible tempest, a dreadful Stations of the Cross. Maybe some doctor of theology will draw transcendent lessons from them, or even add them to the sacred texts of some religion, one of those slightly cheeky cults that always seem to be springing up these days.

---

* This matter of addressing potential readers, as if anyone really could read this, and requesting their aid—well, I didn't plan this, I swear.

THE NOT QUITE DEAD

AFTER A LONG ecumenical journey involving every known type of public transport, Daphne steps down in a distant village square dominated by a huge edifice as squalid as a seminary. (Yes, I know very well it *is* a seminary, and I know when it was built, et cetera; I'm just channeling my character's point of point of view.) She slips into the sterile entry hall and glances mechanically at several crucifixes. For a moment she's tempted, although after the trauma with the Minotaur she had vowed to collect no more. (Human beings and their best intentions are not worth the paper they're written on, as they say.) Then she decides she'd rather get it over with quickly.

Down a corridor that smells of Catholic soups she passes a stocky nun with the yellow eyes of a panther, a type to be feared, she knows. She knows nuns like the back of her hand; she could draw up a taxonomy with a dichotomous key to distinguish the various species of hypocrisy, perfidy, and sexual frustration.*

---

* If there's a theological question, just one, on which I'm completely in agreement with my *beloved* (I allow myself the expression since this is merely a footnote, of the kind usually skipped over), it is this.

She tells the sister why she's there, and the woman immediately drops her Counter-Reformation benevolence and examines her from head to foot, as you do with a shoe that's stepped in some dog shit. Unable to find any good reason to throw her out, she turns and heads down the corridor at a fearsome pace. After various turns and penitentiary staircases, she knocks on a door and pokes her head in with pious deference, whispering loudly as only Catholics can. From inside, Daphne is invited to enter; the nun seems indignant, scandalized.

The room has a window facing the river and a hospital bed that cranks up and down. On the bed, there's a gaunt old man. He's wearing a perfectly ordinary cotton T-shirt with long sleeves but Daphne can see right off that he's a priest. She sees it—even without taking note of the various clerical frills on the night table—in his nosy, shrewd eyes, his sunken yet imperious cheeks, the contradictory tension of his shoulders, the ostentatiously devout position of his hands, in everything. A priest with the pinched face of a Protestant, he's very pale, his skin that porcelain white that shades green in certain rather macabre paintings. His arm is attached to an intravenous line and his nose has tubes in it. He's clearly very ill; you might say death is written on his face. He's a dead man with just a pinch, a tiny pinch, of life in him. And a lot of death.

The not quite dead man has his predatory eye on her and is making small involuntary grimaces of pain, as if even looking at her is an effort beyond his energies. He seems pleased to see her, though. Struck by her appearance, almost frightened, but invigorated. In what is perhaps meant as a gesture of tenderness, he signals to her to sit on a chair beside the bed and with his eyes invites the nun to leave them. The sister goes out, aiming Daphne a look of hate. The unbeliever coughs, embarrassed; she detests priests—especially when they try to act humane.

With someone in this state, you could at most discuss coffins or questions of inheritance; she should have come sooner if she meant to tell him about her string of bad luck and ask for his help. Even supposing that if he were well he'd be in a position to do something, and would wish to. She can't think why she listened to that wreck of a human, his brain fried by lysergic contact with the Great Universal Consciousness, the guy who's never got it right in his life, her stepfather. But now she's in this crappy situation, and she can't very well beat an immediate escape. Fine, she'll stick around for a few minutes. Anyway, she's too weary to run; it feels like she's got three bags of cement sitting on her chest; it's hard to breathe. She needs to get some strength back, and some clarity of mind.

The moribund priest stares at her without speaking, wheezing like he's run a mile. He's revving his engines for his last gasp, she thinks. His voracious gaze never ceases nipping at her, testing her, trying to find out what stuff she's made of. He's serious, grave, a man who's about to buy something way out of proportion to his means and wants to be sure the merchandise on sale is worth the sacrifice. He stares at her for what seems like eternity, there in that monumental priest-factory so unnervingly silent, the good earth all around it nurtured by polluted water and smelling of bovine excrement.

By now he's scanned every inch of her body, except, for ballistic reasons, her ankles and her feet. Still, he continues to train those exhausted eyes on her as stubbornly as before. He's burning up the last specks of life that remain, and he knows it, but he doesn't lower his eyelids, he doesn't give up. It's the strangest thing, though: she's beginning to find being clutched by that macabre magnet doesn't bother her so much. No, the more the light from the window facing on the river begins to fade, the more she finds it normal, salutary. It's almost restful, a relief. *Another few minutes and I'm out of here,* she says to herself.

THE PEDOPHILE BISHOP

THE NUN OPENS THE DOOR and sticks her head in. She's wearing one of those terrible grins meant to terrorize children. It seems she wants to let Daphne know that she has tired the Death Mask enough already. He sends the sister away with a look that says, I'm exhausted but I'm still the boss. The nuisance seems not to notice the gravity of her infraction. As soon as the door shuts he begins to stare at Daphne as if he's seeing her for the first time. Once again. He seems to want to speak, but he says nothing. As if no words were suitable, or he was unable to choose from among the many presenting themselves. Or maybe simply because he's too far gone.

Your mother was an exceptional woman, he finally murmurs, his voice as feeble as a fine cord about to snap. *A very pure woman*, he says, his consonants furring. Until just a few days before, his diction had been conspicuously clean, but Daphne can't know that. Hearing him mention her mother, she feels as if an abyss has opened up under her chair; in this upsetting, surreal meeting so like a nightmare, she had completely forgotten that this priest once knew her mother, of whom she herself has but the faintest memories. *A very fine person*, he murmurs again, rooting around in her eyes with that gaze out of Death's pocket. Before she knows it, Daphne has begun to cry. The way she does, silently, without moving a muscle.

You ought to be very proud of her, says the priest, signaling to her, although she doesn't understand at first, to take the crucifix parked on the night table in her hand. *Excellent*, he murmurs when she understands and obeys, squeezing the end of the cross between thumb and index finger. He looks as if he wants to add some crucial further information, but instead his weary eyes fill with a transparent liquid, a small tide rising from below. After a while tears begin to overflow onto his lined, greenish skin, and fall on the white of the sheet. He's weeping too. Staring at the wall at the foot of his bed and weeping. Wheezing louder now, like a bellows about to break.

Daphne looks at him and weeps, he weeps and looks at the wall. Their weeping is rather similar actually, although her tears are larger and descend more quickly, a faucet dripping. His are smaller and spaced out widely, as if like him they are exhausted. She's not thinking about leaving anymore, she's not thinking about anything. She's feeling very strange, there in the fading light, crucifix in hand, but she also feels this is necessary, it's something like an initiation rite. Were her merciless mental clarity in charge here, she'd leap to her feet and run away, but some overpowering force has nailed her legs to that metal chair.

Now the door opens again and a young man in a white coat appears. The priest makes a tiny—but violent—gesture, outraged that they dare to keep on disturbing him. The doctor lowers his head and disappears. *I learned a great deal from your mothe*r, he mutters, picking up where he left off with some difficulty and fixing her once again in his gaze. His voice is even more feeble now, barely rising above the soughing of the river outside. *The talks I had with her were a great gift to me, I have rarely met such profundity in matters of the spirit*: he looks at her as if for confirmation. For a moment his ecumenical empathy is such that his hand edges toward hers; all his energy is concentrated in that tiny operation. But he lacks the strength to raise his forearm the necessary few millimeters, or even to slide it over the sheet. Daphne therefore reaches out and takes his hand, which is icy cold. She holds it in her own, warming it, the crucifix on her knees. For a long time. It's almost dark, and the river has become a gleaming course of lead.

Now the door opens once more and this time the young doctor is accompanied by an elderly man who walks in with an authoritarian stride. He turns on the lamp on the night table. They don't ask permission, they just take up positions on either side of the bed. There's also a nun with them, different from the first, taller and more in tune with the times. The older doctor has a concertina of wrinkles on his neck; the priest is staring at him, seemingly getting ready to order them to leave. Instead he merely closes his eyes, you can see that the faint light is blinding him. He's immobile, clearly too exhausted even to lift his eyelids. The young doctor checks the IV line, takes his pulse, adjusts the sheet.

The sister who's plausibly a web-surfer is staring at Daphne as if she were a serial assassin. The accordion-necked doctor also studies her with something like bigoted rancor. It's clear they'd like her to *beat it* right away (beat what, no one knows, but the expression is imperishable). She doesn't know what to do; she's feeling a bit woozy. Now she gets up, leaves the room and heads down the corridor, still holding the crucifix. A crucifix she hasn't stolen; it was given to her by a dying bishop. Yes, bishop: that was how she'd heard him referred to. Descending the few steps at the entrance, she turns again toward the river, spellbinding for an instant in its violet hour. And at that very moment she understands that the not quite dead man is the same confessor who sexually abused her for a whole winter when she was nine, and then again the following year. Or better, she realizes that a warning bell inside her head had sounded smartly the very instant she first saw him, but something prevented her from hearing it. She starts to cry again. This time she's riven by hacking sobs, like a woman with a bad cough.

GOD AGAIN

A GOD SHALL NOT and must not speak. The languages of (wo)man seem to be purposely designed to formulate deception of all kinds, stoke up the pipe dreamers, lead people out on limbs and down garden paths. To stir up (wo)man's highest accomplishment, in other words, his/her intrinsic raison d'être: evil. Other animals don't get into trouble because they don't speak and never have done, that's the sole reason.* Divine language is silence; words are superfluous to express harmony and love, or even anger of the just variety. It's enough to look one another in the face, or merely stare straight ahead; everyone will know who's in agreement or that there's a certain problem.

Very soon I'm going to stop writing, go back to being God again, and that'll be that. No thinking, no distractions, no more letting my gaze be captured by one particular thing.

---

* If they did speak, they'd immediately begin to screw around, get fired up, make war. Sparrows versus chaffinches, fleas versus lice, dark gray hippos versus pale gray hippos, and so on.

As I've always done. A god's job is to *show up*, that is, be present, not so much agitate for one thing or another. It makes sense, really; a god that both is and is not would be a catastrophe, whether brazenly absent or merely part-time. Atheism and agnosticism would spread like wildfire, overtaking religions. These are the true cancers of the present day, and everything must be done to fight them. It must never be forgotten that once these false religions are installed, you need earthquakes, famine, terrible bloodshed, or hideous dictatorial regimes to drive them out. That's the sort of shock therapy I'd frankly prefer to avoid.

I have no need of humans; actually, I need to avoid them. They're merely an unlucky accident, a not very edifying sideshow. That irresponsible supposed son of mine created great confusion on that account, he let it be thought that humans are mighty important when in fact they don't count for anything and could disappear from circulation in the wink of an eye. In some ways I'd prefer not even to hear them mentioned; they can do whatever they want, I couldn't care less. I am God.

COTTAGE IN THE BRIARS

WHEN SHE WAKES UP, Daphne needs some time to work out what bed she's lying in. Then, her main processor slowly kicking into action, she realizes this is the room hosting the nineteenth-century laundry machine and the paleolithic honey extractor. And then she recalls why she's here, and her external memory lights up, switched on by that cold shower of recollection. Leaving the seminary, she had waited for a train for who knows how long, mesmerized, staring at the river. In that hallucinatory frame of mind, she imagined the river to be her father. Back in the city, she had wandered around the center, lost to the world. In the end she found herself at the station and took the last coach for the town of the rich people's villas. From there, driven by the force of inertia, she had walked to her stepfather's place in the rain. And now she has no idea how she's going to cope with this day that's beginning. She feels like the corpse of some drowned creature, washed up on the beach by the waves.

Just to contemplate that man of the church she went to see yesterday is to relive a dreadful nightmare. She finds it very hard to accept that the afternoon was not just a figment of her imagination, that she really did meet him. She has to keep reprimanding her brain, forcing it to accept that truth. That it was that filthy bastard, who's probably already croaked—in fact he expired just before dawn, I can confirm—who remote-controlled her childhood and adolescence the way a puppeteer pulls the strings of a marionette. He's the one who put her in those boarding schools where she grew up with the nuns, he's the one who paid for her. She hadn't known it, but she was a puppet. She still is. A marionette come unstringed that cannot be repaired.

Now she thinks she hears voices. Her stepfather's dull warble, in a very loud conversation with someone. She cocks an ear, and for a moment imagines she can make out Aphra's limpid tones. I'm *hearing things*, she thinks; the only person here is that washed up neo-Buddhist who always knew who was pulling my strings and never said a word. He deceived her, and never even realized that monster was meddling with her. The silences and the voids are filling up, the different pieces fitting together neatly, as if her past were that of a normal person.

Now the door cracks open and a face appears, the gay and naughty little face of the short one, Aphra. Yes, it really is Aphra, and she's brought her a cup of coffee, which she presents with the obsequious bow of a maître d'. *I came to find you*, she says in reply to Daphne's evident astonishment. She's clearly very pleased to have surprised her, and pleased to share her happiness. But the beanpole is paralyzed. To have something to hold onto, she takes the cup in hand and conveys it to her lips. It's very good this coffee, she thinks, it's just what she needs. She smiles, unable not to smile, although she thinks she might be a character in a video game. Aphra sits on the edge of the bed, looks at her. *Your stepfather is a gas, he just slays me*, she says. She smiles. Her gum-colored gums and her very white teeth are showing. *We're waiting for you to have breakfast*, she says, getting up.

In the kitchen the table is set for three, and there are many good things on it. There's even the black fig jam made by the ex-Communist banana wholesaler's girlfriend, the jam she especially likes. And a sort of flaming bouquet of red and orange leaves very tastefully arranged (it could only be by Aphra), lit up by a ray of sunlight piercing the spiderwebs covering the window pane. The air outside is super clean and the sky so blue that even the yard full of rusting remains looks beautiful. The three dogs, too, seem happy about this autumn splendor, not to mention the family atmosphere.

Francesco took me to see a very nice cottage, says Aphra, rubbing her face against the mug of the short-haired big dog. *It was locked, but we managed to get in*, she says, her rascally smile spreading. *There's a nice plot of land attached, it would be perfect for us.* Daphne's gaunt stepfather nods, bobbing his white California apostle's beard, as if the little one has just said the most normal thing in the world. *I'll bet they don't want much money for the rent*, he says. Aphra's looking at him. *It would be awesome*, the little one says, and it's obvious the two of them have already discussed the matter, and what's more, that they like each other quite a lot. This too makes Daphne wonder again whether she's strayed into a science-fiction movie.

Aphra insists they visit the house of the seven dwarfs immediately. Daphne's feeling a bit dazed and would rather lie down again, but they set out on foot, followed by the sex maniac, the small dog having developed a total crush on the wee one. The sky is a deep blue sea, the autumn woods seem to be burning with an inextinguishable fire. This valley where her stepfather lives looks a lot more cheerful than usual. The cottage in the bracken with its worn orange roof tiles seems to swim in that wild sea of thorns and brambles; it's quite charming. On one side there's a sort of ditch with two downy oaks (species information provided by me, she knows nothing about plant life) and in front, a nice clearing with some scruffy fruit trees.

They get in through a broken window and tour the three rooms and kitchen. *Must have been an old lady living here* (yes, I can confirm); *it's a real miracle they didn't make off with everything*, Aphra says (please, easy on the miracles). That customary benevolent smile on her face, she looks around and memorizes various details, making an inventory of what needs to be done. *With a paint job and a few repairs, we can move in,* she says, as if they already had. *Next winter we'll probably need a better wood stove than this one*. She closes her eyes. *My soul is going to flourish here*, she concludes. But Daphne too feels content; for some reason, she likes the place. For the first time the prospect of living in the country doesn't terrify her; for the first time she doesn't immediately see all the insuperable obstacles. *Maybe we really will be living here in a couple of weeks*, she thinks.

They manage to force the worm-eaten front door open and stand out front. By the facade stands a gray stone bench, and a huge laurel tree with the smoothest of bark, like a person's skin. *We'll plant the garden here*, says Aphra, pointing to a wide, flat piece of land between the long-untended apple trees and some apricot trees with bucolic ailments. She purses her doe's lips in a serious frown, for that is where she intends to grow her carrots, turning the soil with just a hoe and fertilizing with manure from her organically raised livestock. *We'll put the beans there*, she adds, indicating a sloping stretch. She's not looking at the earth but a yard above ground level; she can already see the bean plants tied to their stakes, tall and bushy. *For water, there's a little spring beyond the chestnut grove; we need to replace the pipe.* Daphne is a cork drawn from a bottle and seized by the current; she's unable to picture the garden in its high summer lushness, she just isn't familiar enough with growing things. *I'd like to plant some sunflowers*, she says nonetheless, a little uncertain. When she was a child, she was fascinated by the way those gigantic, beautiful flowers sprang forth from little seeds. *Of course*, says the other, as if sunflowers were fundamental. *You just have to choose where*, she says. She seems to think they need to decide immediately.

They're rather touching, these two lunatics, one too short, one too tall, each with her own personal code of purity—not yet faith in yours truly, but still something. They might be some engaged couple visiting the place they'll live in when they're married. I'd almost like to reassure them about the owners of the house—three of them—they're all in agreement to rent it out. Well, one of them isn't yet, she even blocked earlier negotiations with a would-be tenant, but by tonight she'll have come around. I know all the right arguments. And even the rent will be reasonable, the way it can happen when you have a number of heirs. But I'll leave the two of them in doubt because that way, they'll be even happier later. When things are gained with difficulty, humans appreciate them more.

That afternoon they walk back up the creek, admiring the great blaze of the woods pressed down by the inky sky. As usual Aphra tells her a great many interesting things about the plants and animals that inhabit these parts. She darts forward and crouches down, grabbing some beastie. Daphne's feeling somewhat better; it reassures her to think that maybe they'll soon live here and take walks in these woods. She feels as if she's just emerged from a grave illness, still in need of a long convalescence. When they get back to her stepfather's they make a risotto with nettles and other strange herbs they've collected. Aphra shows off her gums and Francesco slaps a hand on the table, punctuating each of his remarks. Daphne decides she can't be annoyed at him; he did what he could. She feels good, and thinks for the first time that maybe she has a family. They had planned to go back to town on the last coach, but decide to sleep there and leave in the morning.

First Aphra insists on sleeping on the floor with her in the disastrous guest room that is home to the washing machine and the honey extractor, but Daphne won't hear of it. So they lie down together on a single bed, thinking they will deal with the sleeping arrangements later. For a while they just lie there, arms laced around one another, glued together, actually, saying nothing. Then the little one begins to stroke one of Daphne's hips, very gently. And then the other. And then she strokes her flat stomach, and then, with her palms, her adolescent breasts. And then she kisses her, first on the chin, and then on the mouth. Daphne, a bit surprised, does however kiss her back. And then, using her tongue and pressing her lips tightly, she rouses Aphra to even more passionate moves. Now they kiss at length, touching each other all over. Then Aphra places a hand on Daphne's pubis and she touches her there too, and musses up her bush of hair. The situation is degenerating from second to second; I can't believe my eyes. Never did I expect something like this. Never. Before you know it, they are busy having sex, with loud heavy breathing and positions worthy of a porno film. I'll spare you the details, but here's the final score: an eloquent three-three. When they fall asleep, dawn is breaking.

MEN ARE IRREDEEMABLE

ONLY A GOOD SPORT like myself could have believed that the human race would improve with time. Truth is, it's been a catastrophe from Day One, and will continue to be so until the end of the End Times. Man's first thought was to steal an apple, his second to steal another by working as little as possible, his third to use the stolen apple to take sexual advantage of an innocent, and so on down to the present day. Matters that start out this badly can never be fixed; I should have guessed that back in the days of the McIntosh in the Garden. Instead I kept thinking that sooner or later they would wise up. I kept trusting in what seemed to be tiny steps forward. Progress my backside: by now pornography and homosexuality flourish unchallenged. Look what just happened before my very eyes!

Their problem is that they're utterly immoral. Always pontificating about honesty and goodness—ever since the day they learned to emit sounds with their vocal chords—and always inventing the most repellent perversions. They blather on about their good intentions and nice theories, write mountains of edifying books—and then commit the most atrocious acts. They love evil, they've always loved it and they always will: it's inscribed in their DNA. No ape has ever written a thousand-page tome on ethics, but neither has any slaughtered his companion and eaten her heart. No hippopotamus ever turned serial killer, no polar bear insisted his race was superior to that of the browns, no cow ever proposed to gas and burn all his colleagues with different noses. Men, however, yes. Just open a history book.

This is not pique, to be sure: I am and I remain imperturbable. Imagine, a god that has fits of rage or suffers, that's all we need! I'm disappointed, very disappointed, but disappointment has nothing to do with being hurt. Humans have disappointed me, that's all. Once, twice, ten billion billion times, and finally I've had it. Whatever some cretin might think, one of those halfwits who think human beings are essential to me, that I'd be nobody without them, the deplorable depravity of that girl was merely the straw that broke the camel's back. Truth is, I had come to the conclusion that (wo)men were irredeemable long before her.

Of course they're taking care of it all by themselves, but I can also give them a push. The way you drop a lit cigarette butt in a dry forest, or plant a kick on a door that's already closing. I could provoke the ire of some dictator so he blasts off missiles left and right; I could simply blow up a couple of nuclear power stations, or design some deadly new epidemic disease. The dreadful wars and famines and disasters on disasters would arrive all on their own, no need to wear myself out. And of course I have great expectations of climate change, bête noire of Vittorio, down there in Australia.* And if I should get impatient because it's all taking too long, there's always the giant asteroid option. A beautiful big blossom, and that's that. It might be the cleanest way out, esthetically the most modern.

---

* However, reader, I don't intend to bore you with his adventures among the marsupials and the descendants of British colonial thieves. When a character leaves the stage he's gone and it would be crazy to put the klieg lights on him again. Is he still involved with the Tyrolean push-up girl from the plane? That's his business! He can do as he likes in Australia, nobody cares anymore.

EVERYTHING SEEMS
TO GET SET RIGHT

DAPHNE CLIMBS THE STAIRS at police headquarters, the condemned on her way to the execution chamber. *The last straw*, she thinks. She sensed it from the moment her neighbor of the Indian prayer-hands gave her the convocation letter: they were going to put her on trial and send her to prison. The fat harpy behind the front desk not very cordially points to a couple of broken-down seats in a tiny, windowless waiting area. In her eyes Daphne's a convicted criminal. The other cops passing by assess her in the same way; they all know who she is and what she's done. They're going to make her pay.

After a considerable wait, a fellow with a feathery halo of white hair tells her to come with him. She sits in front of his desk, her heart thumping wildly, while he seraphically flips through his files. *We've located your missing property*, he says, with a smile like a sad clown. She looks at the photo in his hand, hardly able to believe her eyes. It's a motorcycle, her twin-cylinder, and it seems to be in fine shape. So it's not about the files she hacked from the Vatican website? Something's exploding inside her chest, and without intending to she lunges forward to embrace the little old cop who looks like a good angel. He dodges ably to one side, his reflexes those of an excellent goalie. *You're very lucky; we recover only about one in ten*, he says, more uncle than cop. *You can pick it up now down at the city car pound; oh, and my colleagues are on their way over there and they'll give you a lift*, he adds. *I don't have my helmet*, she says, silent tears coursing down her cheeks. *Well then, we'll drive you home to get it*, he replies, a pale cherub's finger pointing to her address on the file.

I am merciful. I did not vent my fury as an angry god would do; I didn't have those two bad-girl sodomites run over by a drunk driver, or install a couple of those evil carcinomas that manifest themselves only when it's far too late to operate. I even took care of the rental contract for the bucolic cottage; they've already signed it, happy as clams. They'll live in depravity, wallowing in three–threes every night; it's useless to try to stop them when things have already gone this far. Let them conjure up ten test-tube babies, or clone themselves, whatever they like, it's neither hot nor cold to me. They'll pay for it when the time comes, as they all must.*

The lab director had called asking to see her, but Daphne had decided not to go. But now, as she recovers her bike and mounts it, she sees it's just the time the appointment was scheduled, and thinks maybe she'll show up after all. Now

---

* I might well opt for judgment by sin categories, like the plan outlined by Mr. Dante Alighieri, rather than take up an infinite number of individual cases one by one. I mean, who says I have to?

that she's got her bike back she'd like to; in fact she feels she must. Who knows what bunkum the dapper dickhead will have to offer, what outrageous crap he'll come up with to launder his Catholic conscience, but if he wants to see her, she's not backing out. That way she can say goodbye with dignity to the place that meant so much to her for a large part of her life.

But when she arrives at the Institute she feels a great pincer grab her by the throat. Nostalgia for the test tubes, the smell of ammonia and sulfuric acid, the howl of the centrifuge and the burble of the coffee machine in the hallway. Even for that lamebrain with the purple acne. No need for regrets though, her future now promises pesticide-free carrots and beans— much healthier, she thinks. She turns around to go: no, she's not strong enough to face this trial. Then she thinks (well, she hears a voice telling her) that she must be strong. She swings around again and begins to climb the stairs.

The director invites her to sit in his perfectly intact office, rubbing his hands together as if warm water were running over them. He's like a man who's just emerging from a long hot shower, even more pleased with himself than usual. Here comes a hurricane of *total bullshit*, she thinks; and yes, he immediately begins emitting the usual snippets of phrases that run together senselessly like a mad dictionary. In the end he manages to complete a few of his sentences, telling her that the regional government has come up with some unexpected funding, and that in an enormous *stroke of good luck*, their lab was chosen. And there's nobody who could take charge of this project better than she. She looks at him, as always thinking she doesn't get it. This time she does get it, though; she just can't bring herself to believe it. *Believe it*, a sumptuous, deeply trustworthy baritone repeats in her ear. *This is step one, quite soon they'll give you a permanent contract.* The lab director speaks up again. *This a temporary solution, of course. Afterward we'll hire you full-time with tenure*, he says, waving his mole's hand around by his ear. She hates to cry in front of the big dickhead, but she starts to cry. Now he too is moved, his eyes fill for an instant. He seems to have forgotten that he was the one who cheated her out of a job.

Now you might think it was I who took care of this matter, too, but no, I didn't lift a finger. The dying bishop did it. Somehow he figured out why she was there, and summoning his strength for the last time, he put through a call to a certain senator, who then called the director of the Institute (a man appointed by the senator's own political party), and by 9 p.m. that evening, all was settled. The powerful senator and fierce opponent of gay marriage sent word to the pedophile bishop that the beanpole would be given a permanent job in a few months, because one had opened up. The bishop could no longer speak, he already had more than a foot in the tomb, but he shook his head ever so slightly. Then he shook it again to request extreme unction.

Unfortunately something very sad has happened, the director tells her as he walks her to the stairs, beating both arms in the air as if chasing away Mendelian fruit flies. *The candidate to whom we offered the job was knocked down by a truck at a zebra crossing*, he goes on, marshaling the usual stumps of phrases, limbs lopped off by an overzealous gardener. The doctors couldn't say whether she would come out of the coma (yes, she will) and whether, if she did, there would be any brain injury (impossible to rule out some aftereffects), in any case she wouldn't be returning to the job. *Dreadful bad luck, the truck was actually going extremely slowly,* he says, getting slightly teary again thinking how easily it could have happened to him, who's always so distracted. *God disposes, in his infinite wisdom,* he sighs. I can only confirm that.

Ms. Einstein is sorry that the stupid showgirl's in a coma, but she's practically flying as she leaves the Institute. The force of gravity has diminished and her lungs seem full of nitrous oxide, that funny gas that pulls her lips to the sides of her mouth, making her smile. The threadbare estate which houses the institute looks beautiful today, and the blackbirds are winking at her. She'll return to work tomorrow, she thinks. Then she reconsiders. Next Monday morning will do fine. Now that she knows she'll have some kind of salary, even if modest, she can look for a studio apartment (she'll find one, trust me). She certainly means to live with Aphra (*man of my life,* she thinks), but right now she'd prefer to have a base in the city so that she doesn't have to commute to and from work every day, among other things. She mounts her bike and as she rides home she's floating on air, an archangel on the ceiling of some damn church.

EXTINCTION

UP UNTIL NOW, my infinite goodness has prevailed. But the time has come to extinguish them, men. Humans. As I did with dinosaurs, with mammoths, each time sweeping a goodly number of creatures off the planet. And I have no regrets. After a while you can get fed up with a species, like everything else. You want to see new faces, you need fresh air. Not to mention the fact that (wo)men are wiping out a stratospheric number of plants and animals at an ever-crazier rate. Extinguishing them will be a genuine ecological good deed. If you think about it, they are merely a single species among ten million in the animal kingdom (I disregard their unreliable estimates). The difference between 9,999,999 and 10 million changes little, I think you'll agree. Very soon now, perhaps even as I write the final syllable of this fatal diary, I'll pull the switch, and they'll get what they deserve.

Yes, it will be some time before all the traces of their misdeeds disappear, but it's important to begin. The rivers will begin to run where they desire to run, properly flooding the plains. Highways and cities will disappear under a tangle of vegetation. First moss and lichens will spread, then grasses, then mighty oaks. Trees will no longer fear being lopped off at the base, or even pruned; they'll tower undisturbed again. In short, I trust in the vegetable world to repair things. At the most I might spread a little fertilizer—organic, of course; we've had enough chemistry. The skyscrapers will begin to lean like the Leaning Tower of Pisa (Pizza?), then they'll all topple over like bowling pins. Farewell paved parking lots, high-tension lines, shopping centers, airports: the forests will rule every-where. Above all, no more churches, those dangerous dens of hypocrisy. I can't wait to be free of them again.

How peaceful it will be without (wo)men; I can already taste the deep serenity. No more airplanes deafening the atmos-phere—and covering the sky with those unsightly trails—no more smelly industries and exhaust pipes, no more carloads of carbon dioxide. Fish will be free to tear around the sea without fear of ending up in a can, or as fish meal in a pigpen. Birds will fly where they wish, cows will stop producing that poor-quality milk and slowly relearn how to be less *tame*. Dogs will shed that intolerable servile air, cats will scratch and hiss again. Free competition among the species will be re-established, minus those tricks and cheap shots human beings have always imposed to their own advantage.

The only thing that could go wrong would be if a few cun-ning survivors were to remain hidden away in some cave or swamp. There they'd be, quiet as mice, gnawing on wild berries and lizards, awaiting better times, until they could carry out one of their demographic explosions, a skill they're unequaled at, lying low the way a half-forgotten epidemic disease does, and then suddenly multiplying aggressively, like a bomb going off. I wouldn't be at all surprised if in less than no time they'd have reinvented fire, iron blades, gunpowder, and so forth down to cell phones. So I'll be keeping an eye trained to be sure not even the tiniest pocket of resistance survives. If necessary, I'll employ a powerful volcano, one of those emitting cinders of lava that darken the sky for several years, a Pompeii 2.0. I have no intention of repeating this foolish comedy.

Come to think of it, the best solution might be to give Andromeda a push, like you do a child on a swing, to speed her up. The apocalyptic collision is predicted in two billion years? How about if I make that two minutes? Bye-bye Milky Way, no more pointless constellation-gazing. One must never hesitate to think big. Or should I decide something subtler is in order, I could revive the appetite of Sagittarius A* so that stars gravitating nearby, such as the Sun, are drawn inside. I can see that hideous mouth of his sucking in the various stars, a celestial Polyphemus gobbling down Ulysses' men. But this time there'll be no Ulysses to outwit him, no more cunning, no more (human) words. I'll think about it, and then I'll decide. Or rather, I won't think, the right choice will simply impose itself. *I am God*, as I said. And that's it from me.

ABOUT THE AUTHOR

The novelist, poet, and dramatist GIACOMO SARTORI was born in 1958 in Trento in the Alpine northeast of Italy near the Austrian border. An agronomist, he is a soil specialist whose unusual day job (unusual for a writer) has shaped a distinctive concrete and poetic literary style. He has worked abroad with international development agencies in a number of countries, and has taught at the University of Trento. He was over 30 when he began writing, and has since published seven novels and four collections of stories as well as poetry and texts for the stage. He is an editor of the literary collective Nazione Indiana and contributes to the blog www.nazioneindiana.com.

Sartori took as his subject in his early novels *Tritolo* (*TNT*) and *Sacrificio* (*Sacrifice*) the stifling provincial atmosphere of the valleys of his native region and the twisted lives of its most vulnerable inhabitants. A recent novel *Rogo* (*At the Stake*), also set in the region, is written in the voices of three women from different historical periods who commit infanticide. The auto-fiction *Anatomia della battaglia* (*The Anatomy of the Battle*) about a young man's effort to come to terms with and define his manhood against the model of his father, a committed Fascist, and the historical novel *Cielo nero* (*Black Heavens*), deal with fascism and its dark, persistent allure. Sartori's shorter fiction includes the book of interrelated absurdist stories *Autismi* (*Autisms*, 2018) written in the voice of a person struggling to cope with the bizarre, baffling customs and expectations that all around him seem to share. The black humor and pessimism are reminiscent of Samuel Beckett. Several stories from *Autismi* have appeared in Frederika Randall's English translation in *Massachusetts Review*, and an excerpt from *L'Anatomia della battaglia*, also translated by Randall, appeared in *The Arkansas International* no. 2. At present Sartori lives between Paris and Trento.

ABOUT THE TRANSLATOR

Translator FREDERIKA RANDALL grew up in Pittsburgh and has lived in Italy for 30 years (also New York and London). She has worked as a cultural journalist for *The New York Times*, the *Wall Street Journal*, the *Nation* and the Italian weekly *Internazionale* among others. Her translations include Luigi Meneghello's *Deliver Us;* Guido Morselli's *The Communist;* the epic tale of the Risorgimento, Ippolito Nievo's *Confessions of An Italian;* as well as fiction by Davide Orecchio, Igiaba Scego, Ottavio Cappellani and Helena Janeczek. Further translations include historian Sergio Luzzatto's *The Body of Il Duce*, his *Padre Pio: Miracles and Politics in a Secular Age*, for which she and the author shared the Cundill Prize for Historical Literature in 2011, and Luzzatto's *Primo Levi's Resistance* (2016), shortlisted for the 2017 Italian Prose in Translation Award. Other awards include a 2009 PEN-Heim Translation Grant, and a 2013 Bogliasco Fellowship. She writes about literature and translation at frederikarandall.wordpress.com.